SANDOVER BEACH CHRISTMAS

EMMA ST. CLAIR

for Rob, my always

CHAPTER ONE

Ripley almost ignored the ringing cell phone. After all, she was driving, and it was night. She should focus on the road. But it was her mother's ringtone, and Ripley had been ignoring her mom for almost a week. She was one more call away from her mother reporting her as a missing person.

Never mind that she was a full-grown adult at twenty-three. Or that with Christmas a few days away, working at Sandover Events meant a slew of corporate parties and Christmas weddings. With one big New Year's gala left, Ripley had some space to breathe, but hadn't gotten around to returning her mother's phone calls. And her mom would definitely suspect foul play first and ask questions later.

"Hi, Mom."

"Ripley Allister Johnson!"

"That's my name."

"Where have you been?"

She could almost hear *young lady* at the end of that sentence. "Right here, Mom. I've had three weddings this week and—"

"Your father and I have been worried sick about you. Walter! WALTER! I've got Ripley on the phone. She's alive!"

Ripley clutched the phone tighter to her face, caught between laughter and a frustrated groan. She could hear her father in the background saying something, but her mother must have put her hand over the mouthpiece, because now all she could hear was a lot of muffled shouting.

"Mom! MOM!"

"Sorry, dear. You don't have to yell! Your father and I have just been worried about you." Her voice took on a whiny, clinging quality now. "It's just that we normally hear from you every few days. But it's been a week since you called. You didn't even answer my texts. There was that one with the GIF in it. Or was it a meme? It had the man from that show you like who puts on the sunglasses. What's that show?"

Ripley tried to stifle her laughter before answering. "*CSI: Miami*, Mom. And it was a GIF. That's where the pictures move. A meme is—never mind."

"I thought you'd be proud of me for my foray into the world of the internet! But not a word of thanks. What if Nana had died?"

"Is Nana okay?" Ripley clutched the steering wheel tighter.

Her parents had told Ripley and her two older brothers that this might be the last Christmas with Nana. Her father's mom had moved in with the Johnsons about six months before when her health started declining. Nothing specific, but she was eighty-seven. Nana's doctor, whose bedside manner needed an overhaul, compared her to a battery, winding down. But it couldn't have happened so quickly, could it?

"Nana's fine. We're just finishing up *Jeopardy*."

Ripley could hear Nana's muffled voice from the back-

2

ground. "Quiet! *Wheel of Fortune* is starting! Forget *Jeopardy*. It's dead to me ever since Alex Trebek shaved his stache."

"See?" Ripley's mom said. "She's just fine."

Ripley would have laughed except her heart still had that squeeze of panic from thinking something happened to Nana. "Don't scare me like that. It's only been six days since I've called. I'm just busy. It's Christmas, so I've had back-to-back events."

"Exactly, it's Christmas. Are you ready for us yet? We're excited to meet your new boyfriend! Why haven't you told us his name yet? What's the secrecy about?"

Ripley would have closed her eyes had she not been driving. Not that it would have blocked out her mother's words. Ripley could hear the hope and desperation in her mother's voice. It was the same hope and desperation that Ripley felt in her chest, tightly coiled with expectation. Her mom probably had no idea how much it hurt to be constantly reminded that she was single.

Yep. She was single. The new boyfriend? A total fabrication she had made up to get her parents off her back. Just for their visit. Ripley wanted to enjoy Christmas, not hear about all the eligible men she should be dating. So, she invented a fake boyfriend and planned a breakup just before they arrived. No one would pressure her when she was on the rebound. And no one got hurt.

This wasn't like her, the lying. But the planning and execution? She had a spreadsheet for it. Every detail nailed down. For years, she'd been living by this mantra: *You can't control everything, so control what you can.* Ripley had no idea where it came from, but it had seen her through four years at UVA and was getting her through her job just fine.

Too bad she couldn't control her family.

"Mom, I'm actually—"

Boop boop. Wee-oo wee-oo. The sound of a police siren almost made Ripley jump. The red and blue lights flashed in the dark behind her.

No! No no no no. How long had he been behind her? Ripley glanced at the speedometer, but she'd already tapped the brakes and didn't know if she'd been speeding. That wasn't like her, but she'd been on the phone and driving on autopilot. If she hadn't seen the police cruiser, maybe she hadn't been paying attention to other things as well. Did she run a stoplight?

This is why she shouldn't have been talking on the phone while driving.

Biting back any kind of remark to alert her mother about the cop, Ripley pulled her car slowly to the side of the busy road. Her mother's voice was still in her ear, saying something about the sleeping arrangements for Christmas, as panic rose in her chest.

Are my taillights out? Did I swerve over the line?

Her mother had moved on to talk about the ugly sweaters she had found this year and how she wanted to try a new breakfast casserole on Christmas Day. Ripley pressed the mute button so her mom wouldn't hear her conversation with the cop.

With dread and a thumping heart, Ripley watched as the officer got out of his cruiser and stalked toward her in the dark. And then he was at her window. She pressed the button to roll it down. Her heart only sped up as he bent over. Broad shoulders and a square jaw. Dark, tousled hair and a trim beard. But it was his piercing blue eyes that caught and kept her attention. He was gorgeous, but very, very ticked off. At her.

He was also familiar. He had been a groomsman at a wedding she had coordinated a few weeks before. The couple, Emily and Jimmy, were beautifully, disgustingly in love. It was the kind of relationship that made her equal parts jealous and irritated. Emily had been one of her more difficult clients to work with. Though she didn't remember this guy's name, she couldn't forget his handsome face and eyes that seemed to cut right through her. Then and now.

More than once at the wedding, she thought she caught him staring. Doubtful. Most guys tended to run when they noticed her obsession over details. At a wedding? It was like her normal controlling tendencies on steroids. If he had been staring, it was probably in horror.

He may have recognized her now, but he didn't show it. "License and registration," he said in a clipped tone.

His accent surprised her, sounding more like the North Carolina mountains than the beach. Had she not spoken to him at the wedding? She would have remembered the accent. It made her think of sitting on a back porch in summer with a glass of sweet tea.

"Sure," Ripley said, still holding the phone in one hand. Her mother's rambling continued. She leaned over to the glove box, which was empty except for the registration paper, still in the envelope. She handed it to him.

"Thanks," he said. She reached for her purse to get her license.

"Who are you talking to?" her mother shouted in her ear. Ripley realized she had somehow taken the phone off mute. "Ripley? Is that your boyfriend? WALTER! Ripley is with her boyfriend! Let me talk to him!"

Ripley should have hung up, but instead ignored her mother as she fumbled for her wallet. With no warning, the cop plucked the phone from her hand.

"Driving while talking on the phone?" he asked.

Ripley's hand shook as she unzipped her wallet. There

were few things she hated as much as getting in trouble. She was a rule-follower, through and through. "It's not illegal in North Carolina, is it? I moved from Virginia earlier this year, and I thought—"

"It should be illegal," the officer said. "It causes distracted driving. Case in point."

Ripley's mother began shouting hysterically again through the phone. The officer put the phone up to his ear.

"You don't want to do that," Ripley said, but it was too late.

The cop gave her a look like he had everything under control and then opened his mouth to speak. But he didn't get so much as a word out. Even though the phone was pressed to his ear, Ripley could hear her mother's voice.

She closed her eyes and banged her head back up against the headrest. *What a night! A ticket and now Mom thinks hot, cranky cop is my boyfriend. Just perfect.*

The officer had moved quickly from angry to embarrassed. Her mother was *that* overbearing. Ripley could only imagine what she was saying. She trained her eyes on him, watching his cheeks burn red. Or maybe that was just the lights from his car?

No, definitely a blush. *Oh, no.* How bad could this get? He shifted from foot to foot.

"Cash. My name is Cash."

Ripley rested her head on the steering wheel. *This was so not good.*

"No, I don't have other plans ... yes, actually I—"

His eyes flicked to Ripley's, looking even angrier. As though it was her fault that he took the phone from her and got sucked into the conversation with her mother. *Serves you right, buddy.*

"Yes, ma'am." He pulled the phone away from his face

and pressed a button. Ripley's mom was now on speakerphone.

"Can she hear me?"

"I'm here," Ripley said.

"I can't believe your boyfriend is right there with you and you didn't tell us. And I'm not sure why you wouldn't tell us his name! Cash is a lovely name. Like Johnny Cash. Right, dear?"

"Johnny and June!" her father's voice called from the background.

Cash's glare burned right through Ripley. She could only shrug and look at him helplessly. Again, his fault. She could no more control her mother than the high and low tides.

"And you told us he had plans for Christmas! Shame on you!"

"They must have fallen through," Ripley said weakly. "I didn't know."

"I love his accent. S-E-X-Y."

Nana's shout came faintly through the phone. "I can spell, you know! And I know what sexy is. How do you think I—"

For once, Ripley was thankful to hear her mother's voice, cutting off whatever Nana was about to say. Nana lost her filter when she hit her eighties. Actually, it might have been her seventies.

"Where is your family from, Cash? And why aren't you spending Christmas with them?"

"I'm from Boone."

Ripley noticed that he didn't answer the second question, but her mother didn't. "Wonderful! Well. It's settled. He'll spend it with us. We'll be delighted to have you, Cash. Are you allergic to nuts of any kind?"

Cash's brows furrowed. "No, but why—"

"I've got so much to prepare! Ripley, you better call me tomorrow. I have so many questions. Cash, we can't wait to meet you. Make sure to take good care of our girl."

"I'm bringing my shotgun!" her father called.

Cash's mouth dropped open, and Ripley shook her head wildly, mouthing, *It's a joke!* He did have a shotgun. But she could almost guarantee he wouldn't bring it to Sandover Island. Almost. Her two brothers, on the other hand ...

Her mother's voice dropped to a whisper. "You may not realize, but Ripley has a very sensitive heart. Delicate, she is. She's been single for so long that we really thought she'd end up as one of those cat ladies. Not that there's anything wrong with cats."

"Mom!" Ripley shouted. Mortified, she stared out at the dark road ahead, not able to look at Cash. Every time she thought the conversation hit rock bottom, her mother dug a deeper hole with her words.

"Well, Cash. We'll be seeing you on Christmas Eve. What did you say you do again?"

"I'm a police officer."

"Ohhhhh! A man in uniform! Wear your uniform! We would all love to see that!" her mother said, almost squealing.

Nana shouted again. "My husband was in the navy. And I can still remember how he looked in his uniform. Especially from the back!"

Ripley wanted to die.

She considered speeding away, leaving Cash with her phone. Her Toyota was fast, but probably wouldn't outrun his patrol car. She would at least have a head start ... Then again, he still had her phone. And her license. She dropped her head to the steering wheel, groaning.

"Ripley! Are those make-out noises?"

Her head snapped up, eyes locking on Cash's. Was that amusement in his gaze? "Mom! No!"

"Well, you know it's okay if you do. I'm not getting any younger and your brothers don't seem to be moving on the grandchild boat fast enough. I think that little Tommy might have scared them sterile for any more. But you, on the other hand. You can start thinking about grandbabies—"

"Mom! Goodbye!"

Cash seemed on board with this plan, because he hung up before Ripley's mother could say one more thing. She had said more than enough.

He held out the phone and she took it. Their fingers brushed for half a second, but even in that blip of time, Ripley found herself drawn to the warmth of his skin. That's how she knew she'd been single for too long. After that humiliation, romantic feelings for Cash should be the last thing on her mind.

Ripley stared at the screen. The call lasted eight minutes and thirty-five seconds. That's how quickly Ripley could be totally and completely humiliated.

She didn't want to look back at Cash. How was she going to explain it to her family when he didn't actually show up for Christmas? Why had she thought lying about a boyfriend was a good idea? This did not fit in with her spreadsheet. Not at all.

And how was she going to explain her family to the very handsome police officer still standing outside her car?

"I'm so sorry," Ripley said, still not looking at Cash. "My mother is ... just ... I'm sorry. About all of that."

She threw the phone in her purse and clamped her hands around the steering wheel, waiting for his reaction. But he didn't speak. She finally let her eyes drift up to his face. Cash still held on to her license and registration. His eyes were unreadable, but they didn't look any less intimidating after her apology. If anything, his irritation level had jumped up from a six and a half to a solid nine.

"You don't have to come for Christmas Eve dinner," she went on, hoping he would hand her back her documents and be on his way. "Obviously. I lied to them about having a boyfriend so they'd stop asking. I planned to break up with him before they got here."

For a moment, there was only silence. "What kind of person breaks up with someone right before Christmas?"

Ripley could only stare. Why did he sound so angry?

She spoke slowly, just in case he didn't understand. "Well, it's a fake boyfriend. And if I said he broke up with me, I'd have to pretend to be all sad. I wanted to have a nice holiday with my family. This will keep them from bugging me about being single or trying to set me up. It's the perfect solution to an overbearing family. Except for the whole lying part."

She winced. That was the only flaw in her plan. And, as evidenced by how the last ten minutes had gone, it was a big one.

"So, you just ditch your boyfriend at a time that's already very emotionally difficult for people?"

Now he sounded disgusted with her. As if she would really break up with someone right before Christmas!

It was Ripley's turn to get angry. He might be able to tell her how to drive, but he didn't get to tell her how to handle her family or her pretend relationship.

"My fake, pretend, nonexistent boyfriend. Anyway, it doesn't concern you. You and I aren't really dating. Or fake dating."

"Of course not."

Oh, so now she wasn't good enough for him, fake or otherwise? His scoffing tone infuriated her.

She opened her mouth to say something else, but he cut in. "License and registration."

"They're in your hand!" That came out a little more shout-y than she meant for it to. This whole night was turning into a massive headache of variables she couldn't control.

He looked down where the registration was now crumpled in his fist. "Right." Spinning on his heel, he walked back to his cruiser.

Her cheeks burned. The nerve of this guy! To knock her choices about a fake boyfriend after butting in on a phone call with her mother. And now he was going to give her a ticket on top of it? Classy.

Her fingers itched to call someone about this and complain. She didn't have a lot of friends since she moved here in May. Co-workers she liked, but no real friends. Why was it so hard to make friends after graduating? It really was.

She thought about calling her best friend. Abby would love this story. But talking on the phone while waiting for him to write her a ticket or a warning seemed like a bad plan. Instead, she rested her forehead on the steering wheel again, wishing Cash would hurry.

When he appeared at her window, Ripley sat up and met his gaze again. Man, he was handsome. Too bad they met like this instead of some normal way. Would it all have gone so wrong? She shook off that thought. He was a jerk, plain and simple. Then again, he had been put into a ridiculous position by Ripley's mother. He was probably in shock.

She softened slightly, sighing before she spoke. "Look. I'm sorry again for getting you involved in this mess. My mom is so pushy. Just don't worry about it, okay?"

"My mom was pretty pushy too," he said.

Was? He looked surprised that he had even said the

words, but the look quickly morphed back into the cool hardness she was getting used to. Cash handed her license, registration, and a ticket through her window.

"A ticket?"

He shrugged. "You were going ten over. Maybe next time, consider saving your phone calls for when you aren't driving. It may not be illegal, but clearly you need all your focus on the road."

Ripley just blinked at him, holding the ticket in her hand.

And then Cash spun on his heel and made his way back to his cruiser. Before she could even start her car again, he pulled away. Ripley watched his taillights disappear ahead of her.

Merry Christmas to me.

The whole way home, her anger simmered as she replayed their conversation. Each time made her angrier. One thing she knew: breaking up with her fake boyfriend was going to feel a lot more satisfying now as she pictured Cash's face.

CHAPTER TWO

C ash was starting to hate breakfast.

Not the food part of breakfast. He was partial to waffles with butter, along with bacon and what his father had always called runny eggs. Sunny-side-up was the term Cash used when ordering, but in his head, they were always runny eggs.

No, he had no problem with breakfast foods. It was the *company*. Specifically, the three other guys he met with for what Beau had named Bible & Breakfast. Which this past nine or so months had morphed into what Cash thought of as Talk about Our Ladies Breakfast. Their Ladies, to be more accurate. Cash was the only one of the four not married or engaged.

So, yeah. He was starting to hate breakfast.

"How was the honeymoon, man?" Beau clapped a hand on Jimmy's shoulder as he sat down at the booth. The two of them could have been brothers with their broad shoulders and tousled blond hair. They definitely looked like guys who lived at the beach. The booth could hardly contain them.

Cash was equally as squished on his side next to Jackson. At least he had the outside so he could stretch his legs a bit.

"Two weeks on an island with Emily? It was epic." Jimmy grinned, his eyes looking slightly glazed, as though images from the honeymoon played through his thoughts.

"You already live on an island with Emily," Jackson said, chuckling.

"True. I guess getting to a different island made it feel new somehow. Or the getting married part. Either way, I'm happy to report that the first two weeks of marriage have been great."

"Just wait," Jackson said. "It will only get better."

And then the next five or ten years will make you wish you'd never gotten married.

Cash managed to keep his eye roll to himself and tried to shove down the chorus of negativity in his head. The wedding had been two weeks before. Jimmy didn't need to hear Cash's thoughts about how easily vows could be broken. About how quickly the honeymoon could end, leaving him broken and hurting, wondering where it all went wrong. In fact, it was good for Cash to have this reminder.

After pulling over Ripley two nights ago, his thoughts had been invaded by the pretty blonde. It wasn't the first time, either. At Jimmy's rehearsal dinner and wedding, the event planner had caught his eye. He found himself admiring her, despite his best efforts not to. Now, the attraction had been tempered with equal parts irritation, but that only seemed to keep his mind circling back to her.

Talking on the phone while driving was strike one. And lying to her parents about having a boyfriend? It had been the opposite of how he saw her at the wedding, where she had been cool, calm, controlled. But lying to her parents confirmed his opinions on women: they weren't to be trusted.

So why couldn't he stop picturing her green eyes?

Jackson nudged Cash, giving him a questioning look with his eyebrows raised. Cash sighed, pushing Ripley back out of his thoughts, and gave a small nod as if to say, *I'm fine.*

By now, the guys were all used to Cash's pessimistic view of love, even if he hadn't shared—and wouldn't share—why. His story was the kind that would shut down any and all conversation. It sounded more like a soap opera storyline than real life. That's how he preferred to think of it, actually. Fiction. Not his real life.

The guys probably thought he was just bitter because he was the only single one. Cash had watched Jackson and now Jimmy get married this past year. Beau had proposed to Mercer but not yet set a date. It wouldn't be long. And then Cash would be the only holdout. The seventh wheel for good. It wasn't that he didn't like the women his friends were with, but more that he didn't trust relationships period. Or the idea of love.

"I'm happy for you," Cash managed to say. Thankfully, the food arrived, allowing him an easy out as the conversation continued around him. Cash spread butter over his waffle and took small bites, chewing longer than he needed. Anything to keep him from speaking up and raining on the love parade.

As though reading his thoughts, Beau asked, "Are you heading home for Christmas, Cash?"

"Nope." He hadn't returned home since he left two years before and didn't plan to. Ever. No matter how many times his father called. He'd even enlisted Olivia to call and text recently. As though Cash would be any more likely to pick up for his *stepmother*. That was the right term, technically. But he would never be able to even think it without a sneer.

"You're welcome to spend the day with me and Jenna," Jackson said. "Her sister and family are coming down on Christmas Day. We'd love to have you."

"Offer is open at my family's house too," Beau said.

"You probably don't want to join me and Emily for Christmas in Richmond with our families, but we'll be back that afternoon. I can only take so much of Emily's parents."

"I'm fine, guys. Thanks." Cash hadn't finished his plate, but he was *done*. Standing, he dropped some cash on the table. "I better head in to work."

"Isn't it a little early?" Jackson asked.

"I've got some paperwork to finish up before patrol. Glad you're back, Jimmy!"

Beau held his gaze before he left, as though seeing right through his excuse. Jackson had obviously noticed too, but subtlety was more his style. And Jimmy was too wrapped up in his post-honeymoon glow to see anything. Which is exactly the way Cash wanted to keep it.

Driving to the station, Cash's thoughts turned back to Ripley yet again. For a moment, he let himself indulge in the memory of pulling her over. His heart had sped up when he got to her car window and recognized her. He asked for her license and registration like he would anyone else, even though those were the last words he wanted to say to her. Her long blonde hair had been tumbling down around her shoulders.

At the wedding and rehearsal dinner, that gorgeous hair had been locked up tight in a smooth bun. Cash liked it that way too. It fit her personality—the way she ran that wedding with a calm control and precision, despite how far that was from Emily's personality.

He could see when Emily frustrated her and how well Ripley hid it, maintaining a professional composure. Even when Emily didn't hide her own irritation or complained about things being too rigid. What people like Emily didn't seem to understand was how things would all fall apart without someone strong and firm like Ripley managing the details and keeping things on track. She was great at her job. Cash could respect a job well done.

You couldn't pay Cash enough to plan weddings. Attending them was bad enough. And he had already vowed to himself that he would never be a groom. Even if the single life was admittedly lonely.

Despite that, he couldn't help but notice the lack of a ring on Ripley's hand. And then he had the luck—or, maybe misfortune—to pull her over. Still no ring. This time, with her hair down. Cash had found himself imagining how it would feel under his fingertips. How it would smell. What it would be like to press his lips to the top of her head. Or her lips.

Before he got steamrolled by her family, that is.

The parking lot at the station was pretty empty. Getting out of his car, Cash shook his head at the thought of Ripley's mother. Talk about overbearing. Though overbearing often meant that you cared. Cash couldn't remember the last time someone had shut him up that way. Ripley had looked mortified, but the pink in her cheeks only made her more alluring.

At least until she started talking about her fake boyfriend plan. His irritation rose again. On the one hand, he got it. He didn't even speak to his family. Lying couldn't be worse than that, even if Cash felt totally justified after what his father had done.

But Ripley had hit a nerve, first with the lie, and then with the breaking-up-before-Christmas idea. He could see now that it was ridiculous of him to get angry with her about breaking up with a fake boyfriend. But it still got under his skin. Maybe because it reminded him of his mother, walking out on them the week before Christmas. She'd left nine-year-old Cash presents under the tree but took herself away. She never came back. He doubted that she even looked back.

. And then Olivia broke up with him just before Christmas. The holiday essentially was dead to him.

Ripley faking a breakup with a boyfriend that didn't exist should not have mattered to him in the least. But it still sent him back to that first lonely Christmas morning when his father had tried to hide his tears as they opened gifts, just the two of them. He could hear the echo of Olivia's voice as she confessed that she hadn't been faithful. Cash ground his teeth. This was exactly why he had to stop thinking about Ripley. Or any woman.

His phone began ringing as he walked inside the station. His dad. Again. He sent it to voicemail but a moment later the phone buzzed again with a text.

Dad: We miss you. Please consider coming home for Christmas. Or at least picking up so we can talk. I can't tell you how sorry I am. Even if you don't do it for me, consider your little brother.

Half brother, Cash thought, his mood turning even more sour.

"Hey, Cash!" the station manager called from behind the main desk. "Something arrived for you this morning." Bill shuffled behind the desk and then pushed a decent-sized box across the counter. "Christmas came early, I guess."

"Huh." Cash glanced at the label with narrowed eyes. It

was handwritten to *Cash the Police Officer* with the station address and the return from Virginia. He didn't know anyone in Fredericksburg. Where was that city? He couldn't remember if it was north or out west. There were too many Virginia towns with similar names. He picked up the box and shook it, then sniffed it. It smelled like packing tape and cardboard. He wasn't sure what he was expecting or why he did it.

Bill laughed. "If it's something good, promise to share?"

"Of course." Cash took the package back to his desk. He technically didn't need to start his shift for another forty-five minutes, which gave him some time. Good thing, because he wanted to straighten out whatever this was.

With a quick flip of his pocketknife, he cut through the packing tape. For a few beats, he stared at the contents of the box, trying to make sense of them. Only when he picked up the card did he realize who had sent this and why. It still took his brain a few beats to understand.

He read through the note once. Twice. Then, without looking at the rest of the box, Cash stuffed the note in his pocket and closed the box.

Jaw clenched and cheeks flaming, Cash grabbed the package and stormed out to his cruiser. He had to straighten out some things. More like, some*one*.

CHAPTER THREE

R ipley heard Cash before she saw him. The glass door to their strip mall office space slammed open. His footsteps were purposeful and furious. Even before she saw the anger in his face, it filled up the room.

Immediately, her mind went into panic mode.

Did he know she hadn't paid her ticket yet? Had she violated some other law she didn't know about?

How was he still so attractive even when he was angry?

Briefly, she hoped he might be here to exact whatever vengeance flashed in his eyes on someone else. There were only three other team members at Sandover Events, so this wasn't likely. Even though someone should really have taken Phyllis' license away years before. She was over sixty-five and hadn't lost her ability to drive, so much as her ability to care about following the law.

But no, Cash zeroed in on Ripley. And though it terrified her a little, she also couldn't deny that she loved watching him walk right to her. And for reasons that clearly didn't match reality, she imagined him striding to her desk, grabbing her face in his strong hands, and kissing her senseless. Clearly, the whole pretend-boyfriend situation had her mind in a weird place.

He bypassed Amber at reception and stomped right to Ripley. Her blush was at maximum volume before he opened his mouth.

"What. Is. This?" Cash dropped a box down on her desk. It sent the contract she had just signed scattering to the floor and knocked over her mug of pens. Cash crossed his arms over his chest, which looked even broader in his uniform now that he was in good light.

Stop thinking about how attractive he is. This guy gave you a ticket and is now disrupting your work environment.

Ripley mustered her best glare and stood to face him. "I can't say that I know, *Officer*."

His expression didn't falter. "Why don't you take a look? Then tell me."

Sighing, Ripley looked inside the cardboard box. The first thing she noticed was garish fabric. It took her a moment to unfold, and the thing jingled as it moved. With a twist in her gut, she realized what she was seeing.

"Oh no." Her shoulders slumped as she clutched the fabric in her fists.

"Oh yes," Cash said.

Ripley shouldn't laugh. In truth, she was horrified. Humiliated by her mother in front of Cash. Again. But the laughter came anyway. She tried to hold it in. There was exactly zero humor in Cash's expression. But she couldn't stop a small giggle from escaping.

"This is a joke to you?"

"No." But Ripley could only laugh harder. Every time she glanced down, she saw the snowman on the front of the sweater, wearing a police uniform and writing out a ticket for

Santa and his sleigh. It even had bells sewn onto the reindeer. She couldn't be serious while it was staring up at her. Where had her mother even found something like this?

To distract herself from Cash's intense gaze, Ripley set the sweater aside and looked down in the box, a few stray giggles still escaping. There was a container of decorated sugar cookies, a bright red stocking with Cash's name on the top, and a box set of the TV show *Brooklyn Nine-Nine*.

Her laughter quickly dissipated, replaced with a catch in her chest that she didn't want to examine too closely.

This was the ultimate care package for Ripley's pretend police officer boyfriend, Cash. It was ridiculous and over the top but also sweet. And it made Ripley feel even worse about the whole situation. Not just the one where she had a fake boyfriend, but the one where she didn't have a real boyfriend for her mom to send packages to. And most especially the one where she lied to her family about everything.

Carefully folding the sweater, she placed it back in the box. "I didn't give her your address," she said, not wanting to look up at Cash.

"She sent it to the station. Along with a note."

He didn't elaborate, and the note wasn't in the box. Ripley could only imagine the embarrassing contents. *Oh, Mom.* Her parents had been pressing her for years to find a man. And now, Ripley took in just how much it mattered to them. Not because Ripley wasn't enough on her own. But because they loved her and wanted what was best for her. They wanted her to be happy.

"I'm sorry," she said, closing the flaps on the box. "I'll take care of it."

"You mean, you'll tell them we broke up."

There was a collective gasp in the small office. For the past few minutes, Ripley had been so caught up in Cash and the drama unfolding before her that she had forgotten about Amber, Phyllis, and Deondra, her boss, who were all obviously listening. Ripley took in their shocked expressions. She would have some explaining to do later. Or by dinnertime, everyone On Island would think that she and Cash had been dating.

"Yes. I'll tell them." Ripley swallowed. It took effort, like her throat was closing up, aching from the pain that had started right in the center of her heart. "I'm sorry I didn't do it sooner."

"And then what? You'll give all this stuff back to her?"

"I'll probably eat the cookies. The rest, I'll donate."

"Cookies?" Cash's voice softened slightly.

Ripley blinked at him. Had he not looked through the whole box? Maybe he stopped looking once he reached the sweater. She pulled out the tin of cookies and shoved them at him. "You keep them. Consider it payment for your trouble."

The cookies were her mother's famous recipe. They were the only sugar cookies Ripley had ever eaten that weren't completely bland. The royal icing hardened, so they had a satisfying and delicious crunch that paired well with the soft-ness of the cookie itself. Because her mom grew up in Texas, she didn't use the normal Christmas shapes. Instead, there were green alligators, yellow armadillos, red peppers, and a few more. All trimmed in white piping. She could see them through the clear window at the top of the tin.

Cash didn't speak, staring down at the alligator on top.

"I'll just go put this in my car," Ripley said, hoisting the box in her arms. She couldn't stay here any longer, letting her co-workers witness any more of this humiliating exchange. And still worse, she knew tears were only moments away. Her plan seemed so safe, and now it had gone completely off the rails.

Brushing past Cash, Ripley walked by Amber's desk, and strode out into the bright, cold day. The chill in the air made the tears sting as she worked to hold them in. The sun punished her with its brilliance. Ripley almost ran to the car, ignoring the pinch of her heels.

"Wait!" Cash's voice didn't slow her, but his strong hand gripped her arm just as she reached her Toyota.

Ripley didn't turn, but she did stop. She couldn't face him. "What?"

Cash dropped her arm and moved to fill the small space between her and the car. This close, she could smell his masculine scent. He smelled like fall—warm and spicy. Of course he wasn't just handsome. He smelled great too.

And was a jerk. Who humiliated you in front of your office.

Cash stared at her face, his eyes following the tracks of the tears she'd failed to keep in. Without warning, he reached out and pulled the box out of her arms. "I'm keeping this."

Ripley's head shot up, and her eyes met his. For once, they didn't carry the rage of a thousand suns. The softness in them, which looked a lot like pity, only stoked her anger. Without thinking, she shoved the box, which knocked him back into the car. Shock colored his face, which gave her no small satisfaction. Ripley ignored the panicked voice in her head telling her she just assaulted a police officer.

"I don't think so. You don't get to keep this."

Cash fumbled with the box. Ripley grabbed it, trying to yank it away. But his grip was strong. His brows lowered as he pulled it back to his chest.

"It's mine. Your mother sent it to me," Cash said.

"No. She sent it to my *boyfriend*. Which you most certainly are not."

"Seeing as you never broke up with me, technically I am your boyfriend."

Ripley could only stare. "You're ridiculous! You aren't my boyfriend! You never were!"

"Not according to your mother. As evidenced by this very thoughtful care package she sent to *me*."

Ripley gave up on the losing battle of tug-of-war over the box and strode away from Cash. Making a loud groan of frustration, she dragged her fingers through her hair. The rubber band holding her ponytail snapped. Because when one thing goes wrong, why not several? Smoothing her wild tresses, Ripley tried to compose herself.

She needed to treat Cash like a problem client. The kind who wanted to leave the reception in a hot air balloon or have a ten-foot ice cream sundae instead of a wedding cake.

Be reasonable and calm. Listen to his opinions. Offer a word of encouragement. Then present your case as clearly and logically as possible, making him forget his original idea altogether. Control what you can. And you can most definitely control yourself.

Spinning to face him, Ripley fixed a particular look on her face. One she homed in college while interning in DC for a cutthroat event company that worked mostly with lobbyists and political figures. She hated every minute but learned a ton. Mostly the hard way.

"Cash," she said, placing her hand over his on the box. His skin felt warm and rough, and she would be lying if she said she didn't crave more of his touch. "I appreciate your patience in dealing with my mother. She can be quite overbearing. But she will completely understand why you aren't going to be there for Christmas. She wouldn't want you to feel pressured by this gift or in any way obligated. You've been a real trooper and I thank you."

She tried peeling his fingers off the box and was shocked when his grip tightened.

His eyes narrowed. "You're good at that."

"What?" Ripley stepped back.

"I noticed it at Jimmy and Emily's wedding. You can really turn people where you want them to go."

He noticed that? He noticed me?

Heat filled her cheeks again. Especially when his firm mouth suddenly softened. It wasn't a smile—she had yet to see one of those—but it felt unnervingly like he understood her. Like he really *saw* her.

"You're very good, but it doesn't work on me. I'm keeping the package." Cash pushed past her and strode away. "I'll be sure to tell your mother thanks. See you on Christmas Eve." Ripley still hadn't managed to find her words or close her gaping mouth when Cash called over his shoulder, "Oh, and I saw the ticket on your dashboard. Don't forget to pay it."

Then he tucked the box into the cruiser, closed the door, and was gone. He was so infuriating. Beyond frustrating. A real piece of work.

But wait— *he planned to come on Christmas Eve?*

CHAPTER FOUR

W*hat has gotten into me?*
Cash scarfed down the fourth sugar cookie he'd eaten that morning. Or fifth? It was hard to remember. They were addictive. Maybe the best cookies he'd ever had. Right now, he was parked at the beach access next to Jackson's house, watching the waves beyond the dunes and doing paperwork. Possibly because of his foul mood after the run-in with Ripley, he'd given out twice the normal number of tickets.

And now, he was inhaling cookies like it was his job.

Cash couldn't blame the sugar overload for his word vomit with Ripley. No, the enormous lapse in judgment that led him to tell Ripley that he would be coming over Christmas Eve had been all Cash, sugar-free. Something about her fiery response when he showed up at her office made him dig in his heels. It was a huge mistake. One he wasn't quite sure how to fix.

He took a bite of a cactus cookie. Who makes Christmas

cookies shaped like alligators and cowboy boots and cactus
—*cacti?*—anyway?

Apparently, the same woman who sent a very thoughtful
—and pretty hilarious, if he was being honest—care package
for Ripley's boyfriend. The sweater, although horrendous,
couldn't have been easy to find. Cash didn't even know they
made police-themed Christmas sweaters. Yet Ripley's mom
had gone to whatever trouble to find one and then overnight
it to get to him in time.

Not to me, Cash reminded himself. *Not really. To Ripley's fake
boyfriend.*

What a mess.

But as much as Cash hated lying, he could understand her
reasons. Sometimes family made you do things you wouldn't
think you could do. After his mother left them, Cash never
thought he would do the same exact thing. But that was
really his father's fault. He made his choice, and it effectively
cut Cash off from his life.

"Penny for your thoughts?"

Cash startled at the sound of Jackson's voice. Jax stood
outside the open window, looking like he just got done with
a round with his punching bag under the deck of his big
house. Sweat made the ends of his hair curl slightly and his
forehead glistened.

"What?"

"You look like you've got a lot on your mind. Everything
okay?"

"Just writing up tickets," Cash said. "People seem to be in
a real hurry to Christmas shop."

"Planning to go into a sugar coma?" Jackson hummed
appreciatively, eyeing the cookies. "Those look homemade."

Cash only grunted, then held out the cookie tin. Lifting a
brow, Jackson picked up an alligator. "Interesting choice."

Jackson took a bite of the cookie, then looked at it, as though surprised. Just watching Jax eat made Cash grab another. This one was a palm tree, yellow and green with tiny red dots in the fronds, meant to look like Christmas ornaments. He was almost to the bottom of the container. He couldn't remember the last time he'd eaten like this.

Was this emotional eating? Had it come to that? No, these cookies were simply excellent. And addictive.

"These are fantastic," Jackson said between bites. "Where did you say you got them?"

"I didn't."

"Ah."

Cash wasn't about to explain, though he could sense Jackson's curiosity. But he wouldn't ask. Maybe because he was almost a decade older than Cash and the other guys, Jax was better at knowing when to hold back and when to push.

Which made Cash suddenly want to spill his guts.

But what would he say? *These cookies were made by my fake girlfriend's mom and I agreed to meet her parents in two days. Advice?*

Nope. Even thinking about saying it out loud made it worse. Cash needed to back out of this whole thing with Ripley somehow. In a way that didn't hurt her or hurt her mother. And her whole family. How big was her family? He'd heard Ripley's mom, dad, and nana on the phone the other day. He didn't even know how many brothers and sisters she had, if any, or brothers- and sisters-in-law, nieces, nephews ...

Though none of this was his fault, Cash suddenly felt the weight of disappointing her family. And how would it be for Ripley to deal with the fallout? Meanwhile Cash would spend Christmas alone, just as he planned.

Why did that suddenly sound so incredibly lonely now?

"Have you ever done something completely out of character?" Cash blurted.

Jackson smiled, easy and kind. "Plenty of things. Usually when I was in love."

Cash made a face. He shouldn't have been surprised by the answer. A few months ago, Jackson had married Jenna, the girl he'd crushed on since high school. It was a sweet story, even seen through Cash's jaded perspective. But it didn't have any bearing on Cash's situation.

"I'm not in love."

Jackson nodded and took another bite of the alligator, chewing for a moment before he answered. "Well, if I wasn't in love, the out-of-character things I did either involved alcohol or women. Not ones I was in love with, but ones I liked. I know you hardly drink, so ..."

This conversation would have driven Beau crazy. It felt like he and Jackson were having a whole conversation under a conversation. Beau would have tried to drag the full story out of Cash through probing questions. And Cash would have already walked away. Despite his closeness with the other three guys, he still managed to hold most things back.

Jackson's subtext, he could handle.

"I'm not in love," Cash repeated. Even though he knew the words were true, his need to say it again made him wonder what feelings, exactly, he did have for Ripley. "But there is a girl. I've gotten myself into a bit of a mess."

Jackson finished the cookie, licking crumbs from his fingers. Cash handed him another, this time a red pepper. Jackson smiled at it before eating it in one bite. Cash looked out over the waves. The day was sunny but cool, and a single surfer in a wetsuit dotted the waves. That was commitment in weather like this. Or maybe stupidity.

Jackson's voice pulled Cash out of his thoughts. "The

crux of the matter is whether you want to stay in that mess or get out of it."

That rang true. But even as his heart agreed, Cash felt torn. Because his answer to that made no sense.

Cash, avoider of family and Christmas, staunch critic of marriage and relationships, didn't want to get out of his mess. A growing part of him wanted to spend the holiday with Ripley and her family. He wanted to be around family, a *healthy* family, to hear the laughter and feel the warmth that came from people who loved each other. Even as Ripley's mother embarrassed her on the phone, it came from a place of love. He could hear it in her voice.

More than that, Cash found himself wanting to be the man that Ripley's mother thought he was when she packed the ridiculous sweater, the cookies, and the note.

Ah, the note.

If he was feeling drawn toward this messy situation, much of it came back to the note, which he still had in his pocket. He had read it countless times over the past few hours. To the point that he could almost recite it from memory.

It was short but held more tenderness and care than anything he could ever remember receiving from either of his parents. And, of course, a healthy dose of the overbearing, no-filter woman he'd talked to on the phone.

Cash,
We are so thrilled to meet you in a few days! I can guess the kind of man you must be because I know my girl. She's a treasure. If she trusts you, we consider you family. (And whenever you decide to officially become family, we're on board for that as well! I'm a romantic. Don't waste time getting my girl to the altar once you know. Wink, wink.)

Since my dearest daughter didn't tell me much about you, I've included a few things I thought you might like. My famous cookies (don't even ask— secret recipe), an ugly sweater for Christmas morning (that's our tradition), a stocking (we're big on stockings—NO ORANGES OR COAL, please), and Brooklyn Nine-Nine (the humor may be an acquired taste, but one you should acquire if you plan to stick with us). I'll do better next time, when I know you well.

Merry early Christmas! Can't wait to officially welcome you to the family. Fair warning: I'm a hugger.

-Mrs. Johnson, aka Virginia aka Mom

The woman did love parentheses. Despite her questionable use of punctuation, it practically sang with warmth. How could he shatter this idea she had of him?

It wasn't just the note and the idea of Ripley's family that drew Cash toward this situation. It was Ripley. He had seen two sides of her now. The calm, buttoned-up, in-control side at the wedding and then the fiery, passionate, off-the-cuff Ripley. Both intrigued him. Had he met her a few years ago, he would have asked her out on the spot. But everything had changed. He really needed to extricate himself from the situation and stay as far away from her as possible.

Cash realized that he had drifted off into his thoughts again. Jackson still stood outside the window, a concerned expression on his face.

"Anything I can do?"

"Nope. I better get back to it," Cash said.

"Good to see you. Before I forget, are you going to bring this messy girl in question to my farewell dinner?"

Cash had forgotten all about the dinner. More like, he had pushed it out of his mind. After years of slowing sales and a particularly bad stretch, Jackson had decided to close Bohn's, the island grocery store his family owned. It was more of an island institution than a store. But sentimental feelings hadn't translated to sales. Jackson had planned an intimate farewell party with their group of friends the day after Christmas. In addition to the history of the place, Emily and Mercer had both worked there. The whole group planned to go to the store to say goodbye, then have dinner at Jackson's beach house, ending with a bonfire on the beach.

Suddenly, Cash could picture Ripley beside him. Her hand through the crook of his arm, her soft hair brushing against his neck as she snuggled close in the cold. He could imagine her delicate features bathed in the flickering light of the bonfire.

He shook the thought off. "No," he said firmly.

"Okay, then. See you at church for the Christmas Eve service!"

Jackson rapped his knuckles against the side of the police cruiser, then jogged back to his house. Cash piled his paperwork in the passenger seat and then pulled back out onto the road, ready to get back to work, where he could hopefully stop thinking unrealistic thoughts about a very un-real situation.

But he couldn't shake the image of Ripley standing beside him with his friends. Like most of the gatherings with them for the past six months, if Cash didn't bring a date, he would be the only single guy. The odd man out. Whenever it bothered him before, he had reminded himself of his own family and why he didn't want a relationship. Now, though, something was shifting in him. He might not trust women or relationships. But he was starting to recognize how lonely he

35

was. The walls he'd put up to protect his heart also left him isolated.

This whole mistaken-boyfriend thing with Ripley's family had the effect of making him consider something he hadn't ever let himself consider. And it wasn't just the idea of falling in love or having someone by your side. It was Ripley. Instead of letting work distract him, Cash's thoughts instead found their way back to her. What was it about her that had him reconsidering everything? Especially since she didn't seem to care much for him.

At Jimmy's wedding Cash didn't stop himself from admiring Ripley, not thinking he would see much of her again. Sandover wasn't a large island, but big enough that not everyone crossed paths. He hadn't met her before the wedding, and until he pulled her over, hadn't seen her in the two weeks since.

There was just something magnetic about her. She carried herself with a regal grace. Except when that outer control fell away, revealing an inner fire. Now that he had seen her flustered and even a little angry, he was even more intrigued.

He liked the way she fought back with him just as much as he liked the way she dealt calmly with challenging clients.

It was a ridiculous idea, but Cash found himself wishing he actually could spend Christmas with Ripley and her family.

Maybe he and Ripley could come to an agreement. They would be friends. But play the part, at least a little, for her parents. Then she could come with him to Jackson's farewell dinner. Her family wouldn't be disappointed, and Cash wouldn't be so alone in a room full of happy couples. He wouldn't be the only guy without a partner at Jackson's farewell dinner.

Of course, bringing Ripley even as a friend would also

attract a lot of attention. Everyone would have questions—ones he didn't want to answer. He had the same questions himself.

No, the whole idea didn't hold water. Yet he couldn't stop thinking about it.

About *her*. This strong, fiery woman. Beautiful even as she tried not to fall apart earlier. Delicate, her mother had said on the phone. Cash would have used different words for her. Precious. Capable. Rare.

Too good for him, surely. But Cash couldn't stop seeing her face just before he walked away earlier, stunned that he had *seen* her. Shocked that he wanted to keep the care package from her mother. His mind went back to the note.

What did her mother write? Right—that Ripley was a *treasure*.

He agreed.

Which is why, at the end of his shift, Cash showered, changed into fresh clothes, and drove back to Ripley's office. It was ridiculous. A long shot. But for the first time since Olivia, Cash wanted to put himself out there. Ripley might laugh in his face or tell him that this idea of spending Christmas together was laughable.

But a part of Cash that he thought to be long-dead hoped that Ripley wanted him there as much as he wanted to be.

CHAPTER FIVE

See you on Christmas Eve.

Cash's words had been cycling through Ripley's mind the entire day since he stomped out, as unshakeable as one of those annoying commercial jingles that got stuck in your head. She tapped her pen on her desk, staring past Amber and out into the parking lot where she and Cash had fought over the box. Her lips tilted up just thinking about the ridiculous argument over her mother's even more ridiculous present.

Everyone in the office had been busy for most of the day, too busy to ask her about the scene earlier. They all wanted to get as much done as possible on the New Year's gala so they could all enjoy Christmas Eve and Day out of the office.

Ripley's red eyes and tear-stained face may also have had something to do with the wide berth they gave her. But there was a tension in the air that told her they were biding their time. Ripley could feel it, the sensation not unlike the nervous flutter when playing hide-and-seek, waiting to be found. Soon, her co-workers would pounce. Especially now that it was almost time to go home, and the office had fallen into a late afternoon lull.

Low Christmas music was the only sound besides fingers on keyboards. Deondra had made them block off the ten days before the big New Year's event so they could give it all their focus. Three environmental groups that worked with various areas of the beach ecosystem were coming together to throw one large gala. It was the biggest client Sandover Events had ever landed and Deondra wanted everything perfect. Ripley had four folders, all color-coded, and three spreadsheets on her computer.

But even as she made phone calls and checked things off her to-do list, Ripley had way too much time to worry about when her co-workers would ambush her. And too much time to think about the man who had possessed her thoughts for the past few days.

What had made Cash say that he was coming for Christmas Eve? Did he mean it?

And why did Ripley find that idea so thrilling?

Too bad it was all built on her lie. She dreaded the conversation where she would come clean to her parents. And Nana. At this point, Ripley had abandoned the idea of adding on any more lies. She wouldn't spin the story about the fake breakup with the fake boyfriend to her family. She already saw where her lies had gotten her—into a big mess. No more lies. Even if the truth hurt.

She closed her eyes briefly. *Lord, forgive me for lying. Help me figure out what to do to fix this mess I've made. Please let my family understand. Also, while you're at it, I'd really like to find someone. No rush. Just kidding. Right now, please.*

At first, telling her parents she had a boyfriend seemed like such an innocent lie. Though, even at the time, she felt conflicted about it. That little tug at her heart reminding her of the truth. No lies were innocent. And now that her mother had an actual person that she thought was Ripley's boyfriend, the gravity of her deception hit her.

She had simply wanted to enjoy the holiday without the well-meaning comments from her parents and the jokes from her two married brothers. They had no idea how much their words hurt. Ripley wanted to fall in love as much as her family wanted that for her.

Lately, her hope had hardened into a cold dread: she might never get married.

Planning wedding after wedding felt like torture sometimes. Not the planning itself, because nothing made Ripley feel so alive as a solid plan coming to action. More the wedding part. She could only watch so many couples say I do without wondering if she'd ever be the one up at the front of a church. Not that the wedding details mattered to her. She hadn't already thought of what style of dress or flowers or any of that. No, she'd only thought about a guy. *The* guy. The kind that made you want to say yes to forever.

When it came down to it, Ripley longed for companionship. A best friend. A person waiting at home or a person coming home to her, pushing out the emptiness she felt like a poison in her small apartment. One who didn't mind her extreme need for planning and organization. If she never heard the phrase "control freak" again, it would be too soon.

Amber's voice startled Ripley out of her silent pity party. "We gave you privacy for the day. Now we're off the clock, and it's time to spill."

She hadn't even noticing Amber approaching. "Oh, um …"

Not to be left out, Phyllis made her way over. Though she was in her late sixties, the petite woman could move. "I want to hear this too! You've been holding out on us. I had no idea you snagged one of Sandover's most eligible bachelors."

Deondra joined the other two women, making Ripley feel completely caged in. Normally, their boss didn't engage in office gossip, but her dark eyes glinted with curiosity. "Will you be needing our services sometime in the near future? Or did we witness a breakup?"

Ripley's stomach fell. Why was it so disappointing to have to confront the truth of the situation?

With a heavy breath, she said, "It was all a big misunderstanding. Cash and I aren't dating. We never were."

Deondra frowned. "I'm confused. From the conversation, it sounded like you were fighting about your family and a breakup."

"And you were crying," Phyllis pointed out.

Yes. She had been crying. But more from being smacked with the reality of her singleness than from losing Cash. Right? It should have been the truth. But Ripley had a sneaking suspicion that her tears had to do with *the* man, not just the lack of a man.

"No breakup. No relationship. It's a long story. But there's nothing going on between us." Not entirely true. But whatever Ripley felt was surely one-sided. After the mess she had gotten Cash into, there was no hope for anything else. He would probably give her a very wide berth. Or maybe more tickets.

Unless he really planned to spend Christmas Eve with her family as he'd said. But that would be … ridiculous. Right? Just the thought had her feeling hot and nervous.

"Hmph." Phyllis pushed her glasses up her nose. "You fought like boyfriend and girlfriend. There is definitely something going on between you two."

"Definitely not."

"I agree with Phyllis," Amber said. "It looked like something. For what it's worth, despite how things turned out with me and Jimmy, if you can snag one of the guys in that little group, you should. And don't let go."

Her smile still seemed a little sad. It had been six months, and Amber had only gone on a few dates with Jimmy. That's when Emily showed up on the island and the rest was history. It's also why Ripley got to handle their wedding instead of Amber, despite the fact that Ripley was newer, and it was a big account.

"Cash does seem great, but nothing's happening. I promise."

"Not good enough." Phyllis pulled a chair over and sat down, crossing her arms over her chest. "I don't care if it's a long story. I want to hear it."

"Maybe we can help," Amber suggested.

Ripley looked between the three women's faces. They weren't giving up on this. Maybe they could help her figure out how to get out of the hole she'd dug for herself. She didn't see an easy way out of it. That was for sure. Someone was going to end up getting hurt. Maybe her entire family. At the very least, Ripley would be hurt. She already ached for reasons she didn't want to examine too closely.

She sighed. "You might want to sit down for this."

Deondra's eyes lit up. "Wait! I've been saving something for a special occasion!" She darted back to the small kitchen while Amber dragged two more chairs over. After Deondra returned with a beautifully wrapped gift basket full of gourmet sweets and snacks, Ripley launched into the story.

Though they made encouraging noises (and a few disapproving clucks and a bit of laughter from Phyllis), no one interrupted Ripley. When she stopped speaking, the three other women sat in a silence that felt heavy.

"You made a spreadsheet?" Phyllis' lips curved up in a smile.

"That's what you took away from that?"

Phyllis chuckled. "I'm just impressed by your dedication to your plan. Though, I guess that's what we do here."

Ripley didn't feel better after getting all this off her chest. In fact, she felt more nervous and stressed about the unresolved situation. She straightened the multicolored sticky notes she kept on her desk. "Any thoughts? I'm at a loss here."

Amber's brow wrinkled. "So, the last thing he said was that he was going to see you Christmas Eve? As in, he's willing to play along and pretend to be your boyfriend?"

"I don't know," Ripley said. "He was probably just kidding. Or trying to get under my skin."

"Sounds like you should sit down and talk this out," Deondra said. "Call him."

"I don't have his number."

Phyllis chuckled. "Sure you do. It's 911."

Ripley rolled her eyes. "Ha ha."

"You should ask him to the New Year's gala," Deondra said.

This wasn't the first time she had encouraged them all to bring dates. Ripley and Amber were single and had planned to have each other's backs. Plus, she knew herself. Work would take priority. Having a date would be challenging. And it's not like Cash would want to go with her anyway.

"I'm working."

Deondra laughed. "Yes, but we've also got a lot of other support from the various catering and serving companies. You'll have to work some, but you can also have some fun. Cash definitely seems like he could be fun." She winked.

Ripley had just opened her mouth to respond when the

front door opened. And for the second time that day, Cash strode into the office.

This time, he wore a fitted gray sweater and dark jeans. His hair looked almost black, and as he approached, Ripley realized it was wet, as though he had just stepped out of the shower.

"Speak of the devil," Phyllis muttered. "And a handsome devil he is."

Then the three women scattered in a way that made it very obvious what—or, whom—they had just been talking about. Ripley swallowed hard. She thought Cash had looked amazing in his uniform, but casual Cash? Jeans had never looked so good on a man.

Her nana's voice rang through her head, remarking on how good her husband had looked from the back in his uniform. Ripley would have placed a very good wager on Cash's backside looking as good in his jeans as he did earlier in his uniform. Not that she planned to check it out.

I'm just appreciating. The same way I'd admire a lovely painting. Or a vase. A very attractive vase.

The man she had been appreciating stopped in front of her desk, eyeing the gift basket and empty boxes of treats scattered around. He lifted an eyebrow.

"Christmas party?"

"Something like that. How can I help you, *Officer*?" Ripley closed her mouth with a snap. Why did he drag this reaction out of her?

The corner of his lip twitched, like he wanted to smile but fought down the errant urge. "I wanted to see if we could talk."

"Haven't we done enough talking?" Ripley couldn't explain why she felt the urge to fight with him. Hadn't she just spilled her story and agreed that they needed to have a conversation? Wasn't all this her fault?

No. It was definitely his. For pulling her over. For picking up the phone and talking to her mother. For storming into her office that morning. For making a promise—or joke?—to spend Christmas Eve with her. And now for returning to the scene of the crime.

"How about talking and eating? Dinner. My treat."

Ripley didn't miss the reactions of the three other women in the office. Subtle, they were not. Cleared throats, slamming desk drawers, and a laugh from Phyllis.

Cash stood with a face like stone. She searched his blue eyes, looking for a hint of something. Softness. Care. Apology. Desire. They were gorgeous eyes, but she couldn't read them.

"Depends on where." Ripley crossed her arms over her chest.

"Anywhere that would make you say yes." His eyes sparkled suddenly, like he enjoyed the challenge.

She hadn't expected that. Phyllis made an undignified snort, and Ripley caught Amber's smile from the corner of her eye.

"Fine. But I'm driving my own car. We can meet there."

"Given the still unpaid ticket, I'd say you're probably safer riding with me." Again, his lips twitched, but he did not smile. That same light shone in his eyes, making them the kind of blue of the sea when the sun hits it just the right way.

Ripley stood with her chin lifted high. Without a word, she stalked out of the office, not bothering to hold the door open for Cash.

Her cheeks flushed from the cool air, but also something else. Why was she being so difficult? She couldn't remember the last time she spoke to anyone this way. And why did it feel so exhilarating?

It was *her* lie that started all this. Other than picking up her phone, Cash had done nothing to get into this mess. Yet she was punishing him as though he were at fault. Maybe she just wanted to throw the same attitude back at him that he had given her the other night. Or maybe she just wanted to draw out his reaction. He certainly seemed to pull this snappy attitude out of her.

Either way, it worked well as a defense mechanism. One designed to keep her physical attraction at bay. Because that's all it was. Nothing in Cash's demeanor led her to believe he was anything other than a gorgeous man with a grouchy attitude. She needed something to keep her from feeling like this was a date, which it suddenly did. Her very first date since moving to Sandover, a fact she didn't advertise. If her prickly responses were meant to guard her heart, they were doing a very ineffective job. Her heart was already loose in her chest, singing musicals and spinning in a field while looking up at the clouds.

"I'll just follow you then?" Cash called out.

"If you can keep up."

Ripley slammed the door to her car. Cash wasn't in his cruiser tonight but a medium-sized black SUV of some kind. Ripley pulled into the gravel lot of her favorite restaurant. It was a family place, serving American food, mostly fried, and seafood, also mostly fried. Comfort food. Calming food.

Somehow, Cash managed to reach her door before Ripley got out. He swung the door open. This feels like a real date.

This. Is. Not. A. Date.

But I want it to be.

She couldn't pretend to ignore the very real bit of hope

unfurling in her chest at the idea of being on a date with Cash.

"Thank you," she managed to say, in a voice that didn't sound very grateful at all.

Cash jogged to catch up as she walked quickly toward the restaurant. He opened that door too. This time, she only nodded her thanks. But when she brushed by him, her body trembled at his nearness and his spicy, masculine scent.

Stop it.

She glared, and though he didn't smile, this seemed to amuse him. That sparkle in his eyes returned. Ripley had to look away.

"Table for two," Cash said to the hostess.

"A big table," Ripley said.

"One large table for two. Follow me." Even the hostess seemed amused at the odd tension stretched almost visibly between them. She also walked too closely to Cash, brushing her arm against his and giving him a coy smile. Ripley wanted to shove the woman away and growl like an animal. Clearly, she had lost her grip on things.

That's what you get for trying to distance yourself from the man. If you don't claim him, he's fair game.

Despite the hostess' obvious attention, Cash didn't take his eyes off Ripley when the hostess leaned a little closer to him. Ripley's jealousy tore through her chest like a hot desert wind, scorching and bitter. She managed not to rip out a chunk of the woman's hair but couldn't stop herself from giving her a dirty look that sent her scampering away.

Who was this rude girl and what had she done with cool, calm, and controlled Ripley? Clearly, Cash was a bad influence on her.

"I love this place," Cash said. "Great choice."

"Glad you like it. Hard to mess up fried food."

They didn't speak again until the waiter brought out their waters and took their orders. Then the silence became like a living thing, coiled and dangerous as a snake.

"So," Ripley said. "You wanted to talk. Talk."

As she watched, the amused expression died on Cash's face, pulling back like a wave over the sand. His blue eyes fell to the table between them. He fidgeted with the silverware, rolled into a napkin and bound with a little paper cuff. Ripley watched his hands as though mesmerized as he placed the silverware to his left. He had strong hands with long fingers and clean, blunt nails. They disappeared under the table. While she watched, he pulled out a white box about the size of a coffee mug.

"I, um, bought you something."

Every cell in Ripley's body froze. Her heart paused in its beating. Her breathing stilled. Nerves stopped sending their signals, having shorted out at his words. She hadn't even noticed him carrying the box into the restaurant.

When she came back to herself, she tore her gaze from the box to Cash's face. He looked at her with pleading, vulnerable eyes. The rest of his face gave nothing away.

"Why?"

She hadn't meant to voice the question out loud. Did she even want the answer?

"I'm not sure," Cash said. "I saw it, and I thought of your mother."

Ripley stared so hard that Cash probably felt it in the back of his skull. "You bought something for me because you thought of my *mother*?"

With a groan, Cash opened the top of the box. He pulled out a small plastic snowman. Placing it on the table, he gestured to it. "There. It made me think of the sweater your mother sent. Which made me think of you."

Ripley watched as the snowman began to shimmy, a slow dance. "How is it ...?"

Cash tapped at a small black rectangle at its base. "Solar powered. It's meant to go on the dashboard of your car. It will keep dancing as long as it gets daily sun."

Ripley had seen something like this at the dollar store. Flowers wearing sunglasses and swaying in a display case near the door. This probably came from there or cost as little. A small, cheap gift. He thought of her mother when he saw it.

Both of those facts should have made this a tiny, insignificant gift. Thoughtful and cute. The kind of thing you give a quick thanks for, smile, and move on. Yet, as Ripley reached out to touch it, giving it a little more sway to its dance, she felt something shift inside her chest. A mini earthquake.

"You don't have to keep it," Cash said, reaching suddenly and attempting to stuff it back in the box. "It was dumb."

Ripley grasped his wrist with a strength that surprised her. The effect of her skin against his also surprised her, creating a much larger seismic shift in her heart. "No. I love it. It's ... perfect."

Perfect for their weird first conversation, for the ridiculous situation, the care package, the argument in the parking lot, their odd push and pull, and this date.

"Really?"

Ripley's heart broke a tiny bit at the look in his eyes. There was a wild desperation in them, a desire to please. She got the sudden sense that there were a lot of wounds underneath his hard exterior. Ones he tried very hard to hide.

"Yes," she said, dropping her grip on his wrist to pull both the snowman and box to her side of the table. She set the snowman next to her water glass and put the box in her purse. "I love it. Thank you, Cash."

His grin, all gorgeous white teeth against his dark beard, took her breath completely away. Alarm bells were sounding, or maybe those were chapel bells, because her mind immediately went to white dresses and bouquet tosses and first dances.

Wow. She clearly hadn't been out on a date in too long. There didn't seem to be a normal speed setting on her heart. It went from *no way* to *I do* in the span of an hour.

The arrival of their food let her recover from his brilliant smile. But she didn't miss the way relief passed over his eyes and how they shone at her. *For* her. The small gift and her response to it both felt far more significant than they should. Not just to her but to him too.

As soon as the waiter left, Cash shocked her again by reaching for her hand. "I'd like to say grace now. If that's okay with you." He seemed to expect her to argue.

But a guy who wanted to say a blessing before a meal? That was a rare find. Her hand in his felt warm, secure. "More than okay," she said. Cash seemed to have a way of knocking her totally off-balance. He still wasn't smiling but there was a warmth in his gaze.

"Good. And then I'd like to start over. Like we just met tonight for the very first time," Cash murmured, his voice throaty and low like the purr of some jungle cat. It sent a shiver through her.

"I'd like that," Ripley said, surprised at just how much.

CHAPTER SIX

Staring at the snowman swiveling his hips next to Ripley's water glass, Cash wondered again what he was doing here. He hadn't meant to ask Ripley to dinner. When he walked into her office for the second time that day, he planned to bring up the idea of spending a few days together this week with her family and his friends. Purely platonic.

Somehow that turned into him asking her to dinner. Which felt very much like a date. And Cash found himself shocked at how well it was going.

For the last hour and a half, they'd played a kind of twenty questions, getting to know the big and small details of each other's lives. He now knew that Ripley majored in communications at the University of Virginia and moved here to take the job at Sandover Events because she loved the beach. She hadn't made a lot of friends yet but had been too busy to care. At least, she didn't admit that she cared. If he was reading her correctly, he saw a bit of sadness in her eyes.

She had two older brothers, both married, one with a three-year-old that she swore counted as five typical kids.

"You'll see," she warned him. "Oh. I mean, you would if you met him."

That was a perfect opportunity to bring up his plan, but Cash couldn't do it. Not yet. She moved right on to talking more about her family. The sound of Ripley's voice, lilting and melodic, drew his gaze to her lips. He found himself staring, watching the way her mouth moved as she formed certain words. Why was this so fascinating?

"... don't you think?"

He had been so distracted by the movement of her mouth that he hadn't heard a thing she said. What had they just been talking about? "Mm-hm," he said, in a tone that he hoped was noncommittal enough to cover all the bases.

She lifted a brow. "You do? You think that feudal law should be reestablished?" Now, she smirked.

Cash cleared his throat and leaned forward. "I mean, I guess it depends on my social caste. Noble or royal I could handle. Peasant doesn't sound as pleasant. And I will admit that I've always wanted a fiefdom."

Her lips twitched before she burst out laughing. Cash watched the way her delicate throat moved. He wanted to reach out and trace a finger along the soft golden skin there. Or place a kiss right at the spot where he could see her pulse. She slapped her palms down on the table and pierced him with an intense gaze. Her green eyes flashed still with laughter and with something else he couldn't name. The look had him squirming.

"I don't get you," she said.

He didn't get himself either. Shifting in the booth, he rested his hand on the table, playing with the crumpled straw paper. "What's to get?"

"You're witty. Smart. And, I'm beginning to suspect, maybe even sweet." Cash felt his cheeks begin to flush as she continued. He didn't blush often. But when he did, even his trim beard couldn't cover it. "And yet, you bury it all under this." She waved a hand around his face and shoulders.

"This what?"

Ripley looked frustrated, like she couldn't find the right word. "This whole thing. The grouchy demeanor. You're like a grumpy old man in a hot cop body."

Her words took a moment to settle over them. And then Ripley was the one blushing furiously as she slapped a hand over her mouth. Cash couldn't stop the grin that overtook his face. He fought the urge to tease her, only because she looked like she literally might bolt.

"Interesting. Let me turn the tables for a moment. When I saw you at Jimmy's wedding, you were cool and professional. Nothing ruffled you, not even Emily or her parents. Yet, since I first pulled you over, you're like this." Now he was the one struggling for the right words.

Her eyes narrowed but there was a trace of a smile on her lips. "This what?" She repeated his question from a moment ago, a teasing note underneath it.

"This beautiful, sassy woman who can't seem to stop speaking her mind. Even when it's clear she'd like to."

Ripley blinked. Her full, gorgeous smile took a moment to stretch across her face, and her already-pink cheeks took on a deeper red hue. She dropped her gaze, touching the snowman again, making him shimmy faster.

"Thank you," she said quietly. Then she looked up at Cash, her green eyes softer than he'd seen them. "Maybe we bring out something in each other."

"Maybe we do." Ripley definitely brought something out in him. But before he could say any more about it, the waiter reappeared, clearing the plates that had long been empty.

Terrible timing. But it did give Cash a chance to breathe and collect himself.

"Can I get anything else for you?" the waiter asked.

Cash wasn't ready to let Ripley go. "Coffee?" he asked her.

"Only if you're having some."

It was late. He might not sleep at all. But if coffee kept Ripley here with him, Cash would drink all the coffee in the world. "Two coffees," he told the waiter.

"I'll be right back with that. We might have to make a fresh pot." He looked slightly annoyed, but Cash ignored it. He would tip well, and it's not like the restaurant was busy.

Ripley smiled at him across the table, then leaned back in her seat, propping her feet up on the booth next to him. He resisted the urge to loop his hand around her ankle, which was just visible between the hem of her pants and the ankle boots she wore.

How had this happened?

As he stared across the table of the restaurant at Ripley, he found an unfamiliar contentment growing in his chest. Ripley touched the snowman again, and Cash watched the way her features softened. It made him wonder if any man had treated her the way she deserved. Had she never been cherished? Treasured?

Not like I'm the right person to do that for her.

What did he know about treating a woman well? Very little. He didn't have a good example of healthy relationships to follow from his parents. It didn't take a genius or a well-paid psychiatrist to explain why Cash had only one serious relationship. And that one relationship had been the nail in the coffin to make him want to avoid them all forever. He didn't want to think about Olivia right now.

"Here are your coffees," the waiter said, leaving two steaming mugs and a basket of creamers between them.

"Favorite color?" Ripley asked, sliding right back to their question and answer game. She stirred her coffee, which had so much cream that it looked more like dirty milk.

The color of your eyes would probably be too telling of an answer. "Green," he said simply. "You?"

"Blue."

It probably wasn't because of his eyes, Cash knew that, and yet her sly grin had him feeling self-conscious. And hopeful.

"I love your accent," Ripley said. "But—and don't take this the wrong way—you're very well-spoken. I typically associate a deep Southern accent with a little more slang. You speak very …"

"Proper English?" Cash asked, in a perfect British accent. Ripley's eyes widened in shock. Then she giggled, and he wanted to bottle the sound up and play it on a loop whenever he needed to feel alive.

"I did not expect to hear that coming from your mouth."

"You'd be surprised to know that the British accent and the Southern accent are very closely related."

"Seriously?"

Cash repeated a few phrases for her, first with a little more of a Deep South flair, then sliding in a British accent. "Speed up the Southern accent a bit and you'll hear it more. Of course, my western North Carolina accent is not the accent you would have heard in the Deep South where it morphed from English."

"Wow. I never would have thought, but I can totally hear it now. Where did you learn that?"

"English major. I took a few linguistics classes along the way. I find language interesting."

"English major turned cop." She wrinkled her nose. "Police officer. Do you mind the term cop?" She propped her chin in her hand, leaning a little closer across the table.

"No. Just don't make oinking noises at me or ask if I want donuts." He paused, then patted his flat stomach with a smirk. "I'll always say yes to donuts. But they're bad for my figure."

Her giggle gave way to a full-on laugh. Cash watched, enraptured by the way her lashes rested on her cheeks, dark and full. Her golden hair rippled with the sound. Cash clutched his coffee mug to keep himself from reaching out to touch her hair. He could hear the whirring thrum of his heart in his ears. Ripley was so alluring, and not just because of her bright green eyes and the perfect pink bow of her lips.

Cash tried to drag his gaze from where it had fallen on her mouth again. "So, where is your family staying when they come?"

This was getting closer to the question he really wanted to ask. Or, rather, the dumb idea he was going to propose. He needed time to psych himself up for that. The almost two hours they'd spent at this table hadn't quite given him the courage.

Ripley made a face and took a sip of coffee before answering. "With me."

"Wow. Do you have a house or ...?"

She was already shaking her head. "A two-bedroom apartment. Which feels fairly spacious for me. But is going to be essentially a nightmare for the next three days."

"Everyone is staying with you?" He couldn't imagine the family she'd described and he'd "met" briefly on the phone all sharing a small space.

"No. Seth and Gillian are getting a hotel. They're still in the honeymoon stage and he said ..." Ripley's cheeks flushed as she trailed off. She fanned herself with one of the plastic menus. Cash could guess what her brother said.

"Anyway. Don't worry about why. But yeah, everyone else is with me. I've got it all planned out. My parents are taking my room. Chris and Mel are taking the guest room. They'll have Tommy Terror, though they'll probably try to pawn him off on me and Nana. We'll be sharing the foldout couch."

Cash leaned back in the booth, studying Ripley as she took a long sip of water. Her cheeks finally returned to normal color. Too bad. He loved that spot of color on her golden skin.

"Wow," he said. "That sounds … crowded."

"It's not ideal. But I've got a huge work thing on New Year's, so leaving Sandover wasn't possible. And they said they wanted to see the beach. I'm excited, but it will also be great when they leave. I take it your family doesn't do this kind of thing?"

Cash had so far kept all of his family talk to a minimum and planned to keep it that way. "Definitely not."

The waiter appeared at the table again with a pot of coffee for refills. He set the check down first. Cash took it quickly, seeing Ripley's fingers twitch toward it. "I've got this," he said.

"Okay." She gave him a small smile, looked like she wanted to say something else, but then excused herself to use the bathroom. Cash's mind was still stuck on her family staying in such a small space. He had an idea, and as soon as Ripley disappeared behind the bathroom door, Cash fired off a text to Jackson.

Cash: Any chance you have any available properties over the next few days?

Jackson: One. Remember the balcony collapse? It's finally up to code. Passed inspection this morning, but too late for the Christmas crowd.

Just before summer, Emily and some of her friends had been staying at one of Jackson's many properties when the balcony collapsed. Thankfully, no one was hurt, but Emily had been left clinging to the structure. Cash could still remember the horrifying sight of all the broken lumber at the bottom and Emily swaying on a thin beam of wood, three floors up. Jimmy had to rescue her with the fire station's ladder truck.

It was actually the start of Jimmy and Emily's relationship. They had grown up together in Richmond, and Jimmy had crushed on her for years. But they'd fallen out of touch—until Jimmy climbed up to rescue her.

Cash: As long as the balcony is safe.
Jackson: Trust me. I've upgraded all my properties after that nightmare. If you need it this week, it's yours.
Cash: Not for me. For someone else. Is that okay?
Jackson: The code for the door is 5613. I'll have a cleaning crew stop by and make sure the heat is on.
Cash: I owe you one. A big one.
Jackson: Nope. But I would love to hear about this woman. Whenever you're ready.

"You should do that more," Ripley said, sliding into the booth.

"What?"

She pointed to his face. "Smile. It looks good on you."

He was smiling? Cash hadn't realized. Had he not smiled enough tonight? That was hard to imagine, given how much he'd enjoyed her company. But now that he was thinking

about it, he probably hadn't smiled much. "Oh, um. Thanks."
He wanted to tell her that he liked her smile too but couldn't
seem to form the words.

Now she gestured to his phone. "Is it work? Do you need
to go?"

He tucked it back into his pocket. "No. Actually, I have an
offer for you. It's going to sound a little wild, but listen
before you say no."

She narrowed her eyes. "I'm intrigued. Go on."

"I happen to have a house on the beach for you and your
family. If you want it. Five bedrooms. Four baths. Elevator, in
case Nana has mobility issues. Totally free. Before you say
no, just think about it."

Ripley jumped out of the booth and wrapped her arms
around his neck before he could even lift his arms to
respond. Cash tipped over, barely able to keep himself
upright with his arms pinned to his sides. Her hair grazed his
cheek and a scent like coconut and something else he
couldn't identify rose from her hair.

"Yes! A thousand times yes! Why would I say no?"

Her breath tickled Cash's neck and he shivered. As
though suddenly realizing that she was still holding on to
him, Ripley let go, standing and smoothing her shirt before
returning to her side of the booth. Her cheeks had taken on
that adorable flush again.

"I wasn't sure if it would feel too much like charity.
Which it isn't. Just a practical solution to your overpopula-
tion problem."

"Charity, pity, I don't care. This is going to save Christmas. Thank you. Seriously. You have no idea. Is it one of
Jackson's properties? I know you two are close and that he
owns half the island."

"Being friends with a billionaire has perks."

"Clearly."

Her bright mood suddenly clouded over and Ripley became very interested in her coffee. She looked like she wanted to dive right down into the mug and disappear. Cash was trying to find the right words to form a question when her eyes lifted to his. They looked a little misty. Was she going to cry? Cash swallowed hard.

"Why are you being so nice to me?" she whispered.

Cash could only stare. Because he didn't fully know why, or what had shifted today between him and Ripley. Something certainly had. And he hated the implication that she had seen him as rude or unkind. He hadn't meant to be that.

"I mean, I know you probably think the worst of me. Distracted driving, lying to my family." She shook her head, her gaze back down on her coffee. "I lied to my nana. I really am an awful person."

Cash reached across the table and placed his hand over hers. She looked at their linked hands with surprise but didn't pull away. He curled his fingers around hers, loving the way her hand fit inside his.

"I don't know you well, but I can tell that you are not an awful person. Family has a way of bringing out the worst in us sometimes. They know just how to push our buttons. And their words and actions can cut the deepest, even when they don't mean them to. I'm sure your family just wants you to be happy, and that's why they push you."

From everything he'd learned about her family, he knew this was true of them. Even if it wasn't true for his own family. Pain surged through his chest. He tried to push it away and focus on this moment. On Ripley.

"They do want me to be happy." She groaned. "What was I thinking? It's really going to suck having to own up to my lie. I guess that's what I get. It's not just that they'll be disappointed that I lied, but I know they want me to be happy. Which to them equates finding a good guy." She squeezed his fingers. "Thank you. For being nice. For dinner. I had a surprisingly good time."

A smile tugged at his lips. "Surprisingly, huh?"

"Unexpected. I mean, you did storm into my office and throw a box on my desk. Then you fought with me over said box in the parking lot. All after giving me a ticket. So, yeah. I wouldn't have expected to enjoy a date with you."

Cash hated that she was so right in how she saw him. He felt like a coward, hiding behind the walls he'd put up years ago. Walls that were being tested every minute he spent with Ripley. His plan to hang out as friends this week wasn't enough. He wanted more. And she had used the word *date* ...

Taking a sip of coffee for courage, he set down the mug and turned all his attention on her. "I have a proposal for you," he said.

"A proposal after just one date? I think you're the one who needs a speeding ticket, Officer," Ripley teased.

Somehow, her light tone fueled his confidence, her fire drawing out his own. And there was that word *date* again. He could do this. What was the expression? It was just like riding a bike. Except asking a woman out after having his heart crushed and then burned and then trampled for good measure felt nothing like riding a bike.

Cash took a breath. "I've got this dinner party thing with Jackson and my friends the night after Christmas. And I know your family expects to meet Cash, your 'boyfriend.' What if we were each other's dates this week? You come with me to Jackson's thing. I spend some time with your family."

Originally, he had planned to say this much more smoothly. And add a bit about being *just friends*. But he didn't feel that way anymore. Though it terrified him, he didn't want to only be her friend. The fact that he was still holding her hand on the table was evidence of that fact.

The pause stretched out between them. He didn't know her well enough to read her expression. He was about to tell her to forget the whole thing when she held up a hand. Her face looked perplexed.

"You want to be my pretend boyfriend for Christmas? Because I don't want to lie anymore. That's actually on my list of things to do tomorrow: come clean with my family. No more lies."

"I don't want to lie," Cash said.

Ripley pursed her lips. "Then, what? I don't understand. You want to date me?"

He shifted in his seat. "Yes." That one word felt like such a huge weight. Saying it also felt incredibly freeing. "Is that so surprising?"

"Yes. I mean, I've shared a lot, but you still seem closed off. And you've only smiled like twice. Based on your body language and how little you've shared, I wouldn't have thought you were interested in me."

Guess he wasn't being nearly as obvious as he thought he was. "I tend to hold back a bit."

"You think?"

"That doesn't mean I'm not interested." He squeezed her hand as though to remind her that their fingers were still laced together.

A smile played on her lips, though he could see her trying to hold it back. "You are?"

"I first noticed you at Jimmy and Emily's wedding. Not only your beauty, though I did notice that. Kind of hard to miss. But the way you handled all the demands and the lack of thanks with grace and professionalism. You didn't break.

You didn't even crack. I may not have introduced myself, but I admired you from a distance."

"Stalker." She looked up at him through her lashes, a smile on her lips.

Cash chuckled. "Guilty. I remember wondering what you'd be like when you let your hair down." With his free hand, he reached out and touched a strand of hair that draped over her shoulder. He wrapped the end loosely around his finger, then let it spring free. "I like you this way. And that way. Hair up, hair down."

Ripley shook her head. "I did not expect this when you showed up at my office today. In fact, I wouldn't have thought this side of you existed."

Cash grimaced. "I know I can be somewhat of a ..."

"Grump? Grouch? Sourpuss? Cranky old man? Scrooge?"

"Ouch." When he playfully tried to pull his hand away, she grinned and tightened her grip on his fingers. He smiled, which made her grin in return.

"That's three smiles tonight. I'm counting. Are you denying your cantankerousness?"

"Trying to impress me with your big words?"

"You were an English major. Is it working?"

"I'm already impressed," he said. "As for the allegations of cantankerousness, I won't deny that I can be a bit closed off and ... serious."

"Is that what we're calling it? Serious?"

"Stoic?"

"Grumpy," she said firmly.

He blew out a breath. "Fine. Grumpy."

Ripley gave him a wide smile. "Well, maybe I like that side of you too. You get me fired up. But that's not all bad."

"I like your fire," he said.

"Good. Because tomorrow, I'm going to seem like the

tiniest flame next to the roaring wildfire that is my family."

"Does that mean you're in? Meeting the family, hanging with friends—all that?"

She grinned. "I'm in. Though I do plan to tell my parents the truth."

"I think that's a good idea. No more lies or misunderstandings."

"I have to tell you that as a planner, this feels very much like going off-script. A little scary. Maybe we can match up our schedules? That would make me feel better about it."

Ripley pulled out her phone and opened up a calendar app. "I need to go grocery shopping in the morning to stock the fridge."

"I could meet you at Jackson's rental in the morning. Maybe ten o'clock? I can show you around the place and we can go from there."

"Let's make it eleven," she said. "I've got to do a few more things at work in the morning. Just text me the address."

Once he'd sent the text, she tapped on her screen, updating her calendar. Somehow, knowing she had put him on her schedule made him feel both elated and a little scared of how official it was. He had taken this big step, and he couldn't go back now. Not that he wanted to. Or, at least, most of him didn't want to go back. He could still hear that bitter whisper telling him that he was only going to get hurt. He chose to ignore it. Ripley's sparkling green eyes made that easy.

"Great. I'll see you in the morning for our second date, Officer."

She beamed at him and Cash tried to smile back. But the nerves in his gut were swirling, and he didn't know if it was from excitement, panic, or maybe the start of an ulcer.

CHAPTER SEVEN

"You and Ripley. I'd love to hear this story," Jackson said, grunting as he lifted his end of the pine tree.

Cash groaned, partly because of the question and partly because they were losing more needles with every level they climbed in Jackson's rental house. The cleaning service had already been through, and he would have to vacuum again. This tree had been a stupid idea. Was decorating a tree for her family too much?

"A little higher? That's better." He hoisted the tree to clear a part of the railing. They made it around another corner. One more level to go. Like Jackson's house, this one had three floors, but the house was on stilts, which really meant four. They really should have just taken the elevator. Jackson tended to avoid them, even in his own house, after getting stuck in one with Jenna.

"So? Story?"

"The official story is that Ripley and I went on a date," Cash said. "We're ... dating." The words tasted strange on his tongue. Amazing, but strange.

67

"Uh-huh. And the unofficial story? I'd like to hear what's got you calling in favors and decorating a Christmas tree."

They reached the top floor and navigated the tree to the stand Cash had purchased that morning. It was near the balcony doors, as far from the gas fireplace as it could be. A few unopened boxes of lights and ornaments sat next to it. Cash hadn't felt like it would be right to have Ripley's family stay in a house that looked so much like a rental and not a home. Before he and Ripley parted ways the night before, she had mentioned that the only downside to staying there was the fact that it wouldn't be decorated like her tiny apartment.

Cash managed to secure the trunk into the stand before straightening up and brushing his hands off on his jeans. He measured his words carefully. "The unofficial story is a bit more unconventional."

"I'm all ears. No judgment."

Cash opened the first box of lights. Might as well keep moving while talking. He had chosen all white lights and glass ornaments in silver, red, and green. He didn't know what kind of decor Ripley or her family liked, but he figured he couldn't go wrong with classic. Jackson grabbed a second box and they began stringing the lights around the tree, working well in tandem as though they'd decorated trees together dozens of times. In truth, Cash couldn't remember the last time he'd decorated a Christmas tree.

"I pulled her over for speeding last week."

Jackson barked out a laugh, then saw that Cash wasn't laughing. "Oh, you're serious."

He continued as though Jackson hadn't interrupted. "She was on the phone with her mother, who thought I was her boyfriend."

Jackson paused, holding lights up to the tree. "Wait—she has a boyfriend?"

"No. She told her family she had a boyfriend so they'd stop pressuring her to find one. Then her mom assumed that was me."

"Okay. Take me from being the pretend boyfriend to decorating a tree for her."

As they finished up the lights and moved on to the ornaments, Cash explained about the care package, the argument about it, and his dinner date with Ripley. "So, I went from pretend boyfriend to guy she's dating."

"Huh. Do you like her?"

"I do." Cash didn't need to even think about the answer. Though it scared him to admit it out loud.

Jackson grinned. "I'm a little surprised. You've always seemed pretty anti-relationship. To put it mildly."

He had his reasons for that. But he wasn't about to share that with Jackson. Not today. "I guess I tend to be a little bit of a pessimist."

"Well, I'm happy for you."

"You don't think it's really weird?"

"Relationships have had much rockier starts. You know that I tried to kiss Jenna's sister back in high school?"

Cash couldn't help the face he made. "You tried to hook up with her sister?"

Jackson mirrored his expression. "I know. I was a different guy back then, but no excuses. I was trying to get Jenna's attention. And oh, I got it. But not in the right way. At all."

"And she still married you. Guess there's hope for us all." Cash grinned.

"I'm definitely proof there's hope for us all. In all senses of the word."

For a few minutes, they decorated the tree in silence. Cash couldn't stop thinking about Jackson's words. Even though Beau had a position at church as a youth pastor and was the unofficial leader of their little group, Cash had always been drawn to Jackson.

Not just because he had a good decade on the rest of them, but because Cash could relate to his story. Unlike Jimmy and Beau, who both grew up in church and never wandered far, Jackson had pretty much been somewhere between an atheist and an agnostic when he walked through the doors of their church.

This was before Cash had arrived on Sandover, but Jackson still had a bit of a hard edge to him when Cash came in with his own questions. He wasn't sure why he even came.

He'd been full of the kind of anger that never stopped burning. It may have calmed sometimes into embers, but never went out. Whenever his dad called, those embers raged into a wildfire in the center of his gut. Anger with his father. Anger with Olivia.

But most of all, anger with God.

Because how could you not be bitter when your girlfriend leaves you for your father? Yep. that was Cash's too wild to be true story. The start of it, anyway. It got much worse. But that was bad and shameful enough to rock his world, make him put up giant walls, and swear off relationships. Until now, apparently.

He never told the guys the full story. One day, he would. Just like he would tell Ripley if things kept going. But not yet.

The guys took him in despite—or maybe because of—that anger and bitterness. Jimmy and Beau made him feel welcome. He could rage and ask hard questions and be bitter, so long as he showed up. It truly was a safe space. But where those two let him in, Jackson made him feel understood.

Cash knew that neither Jimmy nor Beau had felt the deep wound of bitterness that he had. Jackson did.

Cash's anger and bitterness had quieted. At least ... some. With surprise, he realized that in the last few days, he hadn't thought about it as much. He had smiled more. For the first time in years, he had looked forward to Christmas.

"You don't think this is a bad idea?" Cash asked, hooking a red ornament over a branch near the top of the white pine.

"I think if you were lying to her family and pretending to be her boyfriend, that could end badly. Though, heck, God uses all kinds of things. I feel certain of this—if Ripley is part of his plan for your life, you can't screw it up."

Those words were like a balm to his soul. "That's freeing."

"Yeah, it is. So, if you feel something for her, which you certainly seem to, don't worry so much about how it got started. Be in the moment. See where it goes."

Cash was about to ask a question when a door closed below and Ripley's voice called up the stairs. "Cash?"

"Top floor. Come on up." He lowered his voice to Jackson. "I forgot to tell you she's meeting me here. We're going shopping to stock the fridge before her family gets here later."

Ripley's voice came up again, closer now. "What are all these pine needles? It looks like a Christmas tree threw up on the stairs."

His panicked eyes met Jackson's. The other man only grinned, stacking the empty boxes in his arms. "You got this, buddy. You can't screw it up, right?"

"Right."

But Cash didn't feel so confident as Ripley reached the top level, a little out of breath. Her eyes moved from Cash to Jackson and then widened as she took in the tree. He was

71

about to offer to take it down or even just throw it off the balcony if she didn't like it, when she launched herself at him.

Her arms hooked around his neck and he found his arms going around her waist as her sweet scent made his heart go off the rails.

I can't screw it up. I can't screw it up.

He repeated this in his head while waiting for her to say something. But the part of his brain that knew how screwed up things got with his last relationship kept whispering to him, getting louder all the time.

You are a screw up. You are.

"Cash, this is amazing. You didn't need to do this. But oh, how I love that you did." She pulled back and looked directly at his face. Her eyes were shiny with unshed tears. "Thank you. You have no idea. My family will love it. I love it."

She hugged him again, tighter this time, then stepped away. Cash resisted the urge to grab her and pull her back into his arms. She held out a hand to Jackson.

He set down the empty boxes and shook her hand. "Thank you so much for letting us stay here. I'm Ripley. We met in passing at Jimmy's wedding."

Jackson smiled. "I remember. Good to officially meet you. If you have any questions, just direct them to that man there. He can get you my number. I'm here all this week."

She forgot the handshake and hugged Jackson too. He grinned at Cash over her shoulder and gave her a friendly pat on the back until she released him.

"You didn't need to do this. Either of you." Her head swung between the two men, and she sniffed. The tears were now running freely down her face. "I'm sorry. I'm not usually like this."

Cash couldn't help himself. He stepped forward and

wrapped her up in his arms, pressing a quick kiss to the top of her head, hoping that was okay with her. She didn't pull away, so that seemed like a good sign.

Jackson gave him a thumbs-up. "I've got to get back. Enjoy your stay, Ripley."

"Thanks again, Jackson. If I can ever do something for you, just let me know."

"Will do." His footsteps echoed down the stairs until the door closed at the bottom.

Cash wasn't about to let go of Ripley. Not until she let go of him first. Despite his questions and doubts about everything, this certainly felt real. The way she melted into his arms and fit so snugly against his body. The way her golden hair looked over his arm. The rise and fall of her chest against his.

Shoving that dark voice down, Cash repeated Jackson's words like a mantra: *If it's meant to be, I can't screw it up.*

CHAPTER EIGHT

R ipley couldn't help grinning at Cash's back as he grumbled through the cereal aisle in Harris Teeter. Not just because he looked totally out of place here, but because he couldn't stop scowling and making remarks. As long as they weren't directed at her, she found them kind of adorable. She trailed behind him, watching the stiff line of his shoulders. Leave it to Cash to be grumpy about groceries.

The whole thing felt oddly domestic. And she didn't mind one bit.

"We need Lucky Charms, Cheerios, and Weetabix," Ripley called, following Cash with the cart. She had her list in front of her, color-coded for each person's requests, plus what her mom needed to make dinner tonight and breakfast tomorrow. There was a backup list on her phone. She had it memorized, but you could never be too prepared.

Cash turned around and stalked forward with narrowed eyes, stopping just short of her, making her breath catch. "What is Weetabix?"

"A really gross cereal from England. They usually have it

in the cereal aisle, but sometimes it's in the international section."

"Who eats English cereal?"

His scowl deepened, and Ripley began to laugh. A few days before—heck, even yesterday—she would have found herself scowling back. But after their dinner the night before, Cash's bark had no bite. Increasingly, she thought it was adorable. Though she had been counting his smiles. Last night, she got four. So far today, she was already at five, which she counted as a win.

They were so infrequent that when she earned one, it definitely felt like a prize. And not just because Cash became infinitely more handsome when he smiled. The scowl worked for him as well. But the smile? She was a goner.

"Nana eats Weetabix."

He tilted his head to the side. "Do I want to know why?"

"I don't even know. But I bet it has something to do with television. Nana has a bit of an addiction." His eyes went wide, and she grabbed his arm. "Wait—I was so distracted by the Christmas tree that I didn't look. Does Jackson's rental house have a TV?"

A slow grin moved over his face. Ripley found herself transfixed in the subtle changes in his face. His jaw softened, and his eyes sparked. His white teeth gleamed, and she found herself caught up in the way his trim beard outlined his lips.

Six, she thought. *Six smiles today. For me.*

"Yes. Jackson's luxury beachfront rental has a TV. I think it's like eighty-five inches."

She punched him lightly in the arm. Which was a mistake as his arms were clearly made of reinforced steel under his shirt. It only made his smile widen though, so that was a win. "Fine. That was a silly question. I'm nervous."

"You're nervous? I'm the one who should be nervous."

Her lips twitched, but she didn't want to smile when he looked so vulnerable. "Are you? Sorry. I guess that's another dumb question. They're going to love you."

"How do you know?"

She had a lot of things she could say. About how he had a genuine kindness and a surprising humor. He liked to do small things, like give her solar-powered snowmen and decorated Christmas trees. In addition to the fact that he was very easy on the eyes. Any of those things, though, felt like too much for a second pseudo-date in the grocery store.

Ripley began pushing the cart forward while she spoke. "They have really low standards." It took him a minute. She had pulled a box of Lucky Charms into the cart before he caught up with her.

Wrapping his arms around her waist from behind, he lifted her off the ground and tickled her sides. Ripley couldn't hold in her laughter. His lips brushing against her ear stole her laughter and her breath. "That was a low blow. I expect an apology."

Cash ran his nose up her neck, stopping at her jaw. For a brief moment, she thought he was about to kiss her. She froze. Not because she was uncomfortable, but because she wanted him to kiss her so badly. It took everything in her not to tilt her head to the side to give him access to her lips.

Sensing the tension in her body, Cash set her down and stepped back. He shoved his hands in his pockets. "Sorry."

"You don't need to apologize."

"I overstepped. The last thing I want to do is push you. I mean, I know this is all a little fast. Meeting the parents after a first date—"

"Second."

"What?"

Ripley smiled and touched his arm. "We're on our second

date now. So, you're meeting my parents after our second date."

His lip lifted slightly, but he still wore that apologetic look. "Still. I don't want to rush you."

Ripley felt like all the progress she'd made getting him to take down his walls had been erased. She didn't want to take a step back and watch Cash close off again. That's what fueled her to invade his space and press a kiss to his cheek. His beard tickled her lips. She loved the feeling and wanted to linger, but she forced herself to step back quickly.

"You're not rushing me," she said. "In fact, you're slowing down my grocery shopping. Come on."

For a moment, Ripley worried he wasn't following her. She tried to focus on the shelves, scanning for the Cheerios. Was he coming? She didn't dare look back. Now she was the one worried. It was just a kiss on the cheek. Surely that wasn't too much?

"You walked right by these." Cash tossed two boxes of Weetabix in the cart.

Relief blanketed Ripley's shoulders as he fell into step beside her. "Two boxes? Nana can't eat that much."

He shrugged. "I wanted to try it. If Nana likes it …"

"Trust me. It's disgusting. Now, Fruitibix is another story."

"Fruitibix?"

They talked about the merits of cereal for another two aisles, then breakfast overall. While Ripley tended to stick with coffee, Cash preferred actual breakfast foods. Eggs, bacon, and waffles.

"I can't see you eating a waffle."

"Maybe for our third date, I'll take you to the diner. I have breakfast with the guys there once a week. If you don't want to eat, you can just watch me eat waffles and drink your cream with coffee."

"Hey, don't knock my coffee fixings."

"You mean your cream fixings."

Ripley bumped Cash's shoulder with hers. He looked like he was about to smile, then caught sight of something that wiped it right from his face. He stopped in the middle of the aisle, muttering something under his breath.

Confused, Ripley stared ahead at a banner welcoming Bohn's customers. Cash's hands were clenched in fists at his sides. Tentatively, she covered his hand with hers. He looked down at her, startled.

"Everything okay?"

"Yeah. I just ... really hate this place."

"The grocery store?"

Cash shook his head and sighed. Nodding to the banner, he said, "Did you know Jackson owns Bohn's?"

Suddenly, Ripley's stomach soured. She had always avoided the place because it had much higher prices than Harris Teeter. "I didn't."

"This place put his store—which was family owned for the last fifty years—out of business. The dinner we're going to in a few days is a farewell dinner. Bohn's is closing its doors forever this week."

Ripley felt like a traitor. Which was a ridiculous thing to feel for shopping choices. But after meeting Jackson and being on the receiving end of his kindness, she felt terrible for being part of the problem. "Why didn't you say something? We could have gone there."

"The store is all but empty. Now they're selling everything—fixtures, lights, the works. It's picked over. I'm going to have to get used to shopping here too. But for now, I can still hate it."

"Well, this has turned into a stinky second date." Ripley stared down at her shoes, wishing she was the kind of rule-breaker who could kick over the display of fruitcakes next to them and not feel badly about it. But she wasn't. If she did that—and it was tempting—she'd have to pick them back up.

Cash unclenched his fist and slipped her hand into his. "The success of a date is about the company, not the location," he said. His eyes crinkled up at the corners, but he still didn't smile.

"How's the company?" Ripley asked, her tone light and flirty.

There was his smile. *Seven.* He leaned closer until his lips hovered near her ear. "I couldn't ask for better company. Sorry if I haven't been the best."

Goose bumps broke out on her skin. Ripley pulled back and held up seven fingers. He stared in confusion. "Is that part of the grocery list? Seven what?"

"Seven smiles."

"You're counting my smiles?"

"They're rare. And I told you I liked them."

The intensity in his eyes sent her stomach plummeting down into her feet. "If I recall, you said that smiling looked good on me."

Ripley grinned. "Wow. You *are* a stalker. Memorizing my words and everything."

His eyes glinted, and he advanced toward her. She got the distinct impression that he was about to tickle her.

He stopped just short. His phone buzzed in his pocket and he slipped it out, a frown marring his face as he stared at the screen. After a moment, he put it back in his pocket and sighed. Ripley didn't want to pry, but this was the third or fourth time today this had happened. It seemed pretty clear that Cash was avoiding phone calls from someone.

He said he didn't date much, but was it an ex? It couldn't be work. Maybe his family? He'd hardly mentioned them.

But every time he tucked the phone away without answering, his jaw tightened, and he seemed lost in thought. It was a slap-in-the-face reminder of how little she knew Cash, the guy she was about to introduce to her family as her boyfriend. Because she never did get around to telling her parents the full story.

She would ... probably.

Maybe because calling Cash her new boyfriend didn't feel the least bit like a lie. Then something like his mysterious dodged phone calls would remind her that she hardly knew this man. Even if she was falling for him a little bit more every moment. Being with him felt kind of like a time warp, where every minute actually counted for an hour, a day, or a week. It was the only explanation for how quickly she was losing her heart to this man that she hardly knew.

"Everything okay?" That seemed to be the closest Ripley could come to asking what she really wanted to ask. She tried to keep her voice level so that he wouldn't hear the hope in it that he might share.

"Yep. What else is on your list?"

Ripley didn't need to look at the list but did anyway to hide her disappointment. "Milk, butter, bread, and beets." She giggled a little over that last one.

Cash tilted his head. "Should I ask?"

"Definitely not. Just know that they're for Nana, and I promise, you won't have to eat them."

"Great. Because beet-eating definitely falls under something you do after you've been on at least sixty-seven dates. If at all."

And just like that, they slipped back into their back-and-forth. As though there weren't a million stories they hadn't yet told and truths that hadn't been uncovered.

We have time, Ripley thought. *Lots of time.*

So why did it feel like a giant timer was steadily counting down the hours to an end?

CHAPTER NINE

"Are you sure about this?" Ripley bit her lip and glanced over at Cash.

Looking at his handsome face and the way his broad shoulders stretched beneath his Henley didn't help. It only sent more nervous flutters through her. The same ones that had been there all day, from the moment she saw the decorated tree in Jackson's beach house. Such a small thing, but it felt huge to her. His gruff exterior hid a secret softie. One he seemed to struggle with reconciling even in himself.

Ripley had dated a few guys through college, but not one of them seemed as attentive or thoughtful as Cash had been in the last twenty-four hours. In fact, few of them made it past three dates. They all seemed to get scared off by Ripley's intensity. More specifically, her need to plan and her extreme attention to detail. She didn't have OCD, though one guy accused her of that, as though it were a personality flaw, not a disorder. She was, however, the epitome of type A.

Cash didn't seem put off. At least, not yet.

He studied her face, eyes finally landing on hers. Affection and a hint of amusement lit his blue eyes. "No. I'm not sure. This could be a disaster."

"That's helpful, Cash. Thanks."

His lips twisted in an almost-smile, and he nudged her shoulder. "Even if it is, I'm all in for this. I'll be here no matter what."

How did he know just the perfect thing to say? Or maybe Ripley had just lost herself in the ocean blue of his eyes. Words like that were why this felt like a real relationship after a day. It's why her body kept urging her to lean closer to him. And her heart? Well, forget it. She'd lost control of that hours ago. Maybe around smile number eight. Whatever this was would either be the best thing that ever happened to her or leave her completely crushed.

Ripley looked away, back toward the corner where her parents' car would turn any minute. Her mother had called when they reached the toll booth, which meant they were probably ten minutes away. This had to be a mistake, right? They hardly knew each other. If you counted grocery shopping as a date, which she jokingly had, they had gone on two dates. In less than twenty-four hours. Even if they were the two best dates of her life, it was still barely a beginning.

And now she was introducing him to her family as her new boyfriend. Sweat gathered on her lower back, even as a cool wind made her shiver.

What am I doing? Does he really even want to date me? Why did we decide—

Cash laced his fingers through hers. Just like that, her questions scattered, and her overthinking brain stuttered to a stop. His palm against hers felt too nice to think about anything else.

Get a grip. It's like you haven't held anyone's hand before.

But it felt new. Different. Everything about Cash did, and

Ripley didn't know if it was just because it had been so long since she was in a relationship or if it was something about *him*. When she glanced up at his strong jaw and intense eyes, she was leaning toward the second option.

Tugging her closer until she was pressed into his side, Cash leaned down so his breath tickled her ear and his beard rasped against her skin. "If this doesn't work out, would it be awkward if I asked your nana out?"

Her laughter was the kind that was impossible to hold back. The kind that made her sound ridiculous—it wasn't just laughter but guffaws and snorts and all kinds of unattractive. It had her bent over at the waist, clutching her aching stomach. It wasn't so much that it was a good line as it was a good line from Cash. Completely unexpected.

"What else are you hiding under those walls?" Ripley asked, when she could find enough breath to speak.

For the briefest moment, something like panic flashed across his face. And then a horn honking repeatedly grabbed their attention. Her parents' minivan picked up speed and her mother stuck her head completely out of the window as she waved.

Her voice came out almost like a squeak. "Are we doing this? Oh my gosh. We're doing this."

She smoothed back her hair, which she'd worn down. Cash seemed to like it down. Or at least, he seemed to like touching it when it was down. And she really, really liked it when he touched her hair. This shirt, though—she really should have ironed it. And skinny jeans? Maybe she should have worn khakis. Or leggings. But Nana said leggings weren't real pants. Khakis made her feel too much like her mother. It was too cold for skirts.

As though Cash could hear her spiraling thoughts, he said, "You look great. This is going to be fine." His low voice sounded so firm, so strong. Its rich tenor held a promise even apart from his sure, calm words.

"Promise?" Ripley turned her terrified eyes up to Cash as her parents' van turned into the driveway.

He brushed his rough fingertips over her cheek. "I won't make a promise that I can't keep. But what's the worst that can happen?"

You leave me in three days and break my heart. Forcing a smile, Ripley turned back to the minivan pulling into the driveway. "You're right. Thanks."

"Ripley!" Her mother was out of the car before it stopped rolling. With surprising speed, she went right for Cash. Throwing her arms around him, Ripley's mom knocked him back a few steps. He sent her a panicked look over her mom's shoulder. Like Ripley could do anything to help.

"I told you I'm a hugger," her mother said. "And boy, can you hug. I can already see what you like about him, Ripley. What a man."

Closing her eyes, Ripley tried to will her body to disappear. No such luck. When she opened her eyes, her mother was attached to Cash like a climbing vine. She better not try to climb him.

"Sweet pea," her dad said, leaning in to kiss her cheek. Ripley wrapped her arms around his back and clung to him for a moment. The scent of Old Spice reminded her of childhood, sitting in his lap as he read her *Go, Dog, Go* over and over.

"It's good to see you, Daddy."

"Forget something? ME, MAYBE?" Nana's shouts were slightly muffled from the back of the van, and Ripley pulled away from her father to slide the door open.

"Hi, Nana." Ripley leaned in and kissed her lined cheek.

"Don't you *hi, Nana* me. I get stuck back here even though I get car sick and now I'm the last one to see your new man."

Ripley chuckled as she took Nana's arm and helped her stand. She tried not to think about how Nana seemed to have shrunk since she last saw her. Thinner and more stooped over, she looked every bit of her eighty-seven years. Ripley's heart constricted.

"Well, hurry up, then."

Ripley grinned. "You'll have plenty of time to see him, Nana. And just think—you're getting to see him before Chris and Mel and Seth and Gillian. Where are they, anyway? I thought you guys were caravanning."

"Bathroom breaks, scenic stops, who knows." Her dad joined them and waved his hand dismissively as he closed the door and took Nana's other arm.

Nana's voice dropped to a whisper. "Your father only stopped once for me to use the ladies' room. It's a good thing I've got Depends." She patted her crotch area and Ripley almost dropped the arm she was holding.

Did she mean ...?

Had Nana really ...?

"Now, now." Ripley's father put a strong arm around her waist and they began shuffling toward Cash. "Let's stop with the stories. Okay, Ma?"

"I don't need help!" Nana shouted. "I can walk just fine." She most definitely could not. Despite her protests, she clung to both of them to stay upright.

"I know," Ripley's father said.

"Fine. You never did listen. Now, let me meet this man. Your wife is hogging him. I hope you've got your eyes on her."

Ripley and her father shared a smile over Nana's head.

She bit her lip to keep from laughing. Her father didn't hold back, his laughter echoing against the concrete driveway.

"I'm not worried about it, Nana," Ripley said. "I think Cash knows that Mom is taken."

Cash looked relieved when they reached him. Ripley's mother finally pried herself away from him, giving him a last pat on his stomach that seemed like a not-so-discreet way of checking out his abs. Ripley wanted to give him some kind of warning about Nana and full diapers, but maybe it was better not to mention it. Hopefully, they made those Depends really well.

"Cash, this is my nana. Nana, this is my ... This is Cash."

Maybe it was cowardly or maybe simply being cautious, but she couldn't call Cash her boyfriend. It wasn't that it felt like a lie, but more that she didn't fully believe it.

Or maybe because she wanted it to be true too much. Saying it out loud felt like it might jinx the whole thing.

For his part, Cash didn't seem fazed by her awkwardness. "Nice to meet you, ma'am."

Nana straightened up and held out her hand, clearly meant to be kissed, not shaken. Ripley tried to remind herself that she didn't need to be embarrassed by her family's behavior. She couldn't control them. Not even if she wanted to. And Cash agreed to this. It wasn't like he didn't know. From the first phone call to the care package, he had been warned.

When Cash lifted Nana's hand to his lips and pressed a kiss there, warmth flooded Ripley's belly. The gesture was meant to charm Nana, but it worked on her just as well. At a glance, Cash looked like a tough, strong man. But he had a tenderness to him and a sweetness that she suspected not many people got to see. She felt lucky to be one of the few.

"You may call me Eloise," Nana said, her soft cheeks

turning pink. "And before you ask, I'm much too old for you."

Cash grinned. "I can see where Ripley gets her beauty from. And her fire." His glance moved from Nana to Ripley's mother, who giggled and fluffed her shoulder-length gray hair.

Ripley realized she was grinning at Cash like a fool. It had not gone without notice. Both her parents and Nana were grinning right back, looking between Ripley and Cash. He looked like the cat who ate the cream. So much for playing it cool about her new boyfriend. On the plus side, there was no need to sell them on their relationship.

"Nana, didn't you need the bathroom? Let's get you upstairs. We can come back for the bags later. The elevator is over here."

"Elevator? How much are they paying you to work at weddings? This is like one of the Kardashians' houses," Nana said.

Ripley could hear Cash chuckling behind her. "This house belongs to one of Cash's friends. He owns a lot of rental properties. This one happened to be open this week and so he offered it to us. And why are you watching the Kardashians?"

Ripley was scared of the answer, but Nana didn't seem to hear the question.

"Right on the beach? This friend of Cash's must be filthy rich. Not that I mind a wealthy man."

"He grew up here and his father started a development company before Sandover became a tourist destination. He's done well," Cash said.

"I'll say. Make sure you introduce me. Is he single?"

"Nana!" Ripley couldn't look at Cash.

But he chuckled. "Nope. Got married earlier this year."

"Too bad. The good ones are always taken." The elevator dinged. "Is this thing safe? It's tiny!"

"Safe but slow," Cash assured her, putting a hand on the door to keep it open.

It was small. Definitely not big enough for all of them. Ripley's mother pushed past her and took Nana's arm. "You young people can take the stairs. In case you need privacy for any reason," she said, shooing Ripley away with a wink.

Her cheeks went pink. "The main area is on the third floor!" Ripley called as the elevator doors began to close. She pulled Cash's hand toward the stairs.

"No need to rush," he said. "That thing will take like ten minutes to get up to the top."

Even so, he didn't let go of her hand, but laced their fingers together as they started up the steps to the first level. He had been doing that a lot today. It felt both familiar and also new enough that every time he did it, she felt the heat travel up her arm and straight to the center of her chest.

Ripley couldn't say she minded. Not a bit. But it worried her. Every moment with him seemed to solidify her feelings into something very real. He seemed to feel the same way. Could she trust this? Trust him?

"Nana's really something." She almost didn't want to look at Cash. But when she did, his eyes were so full of mischief that she elbowed him in the side.

Ripley groaned. "Will you come to my funeral?"

Cash's brows knit together. "Are you ... okay?"

"I'm pretty sure that I'm going to die of embarrassment sometime in the next two days."

Cash pulled her around to face him. She was surprised by the earnestness in his face.

"Don't be embarrassed by your family. They are quirky and a little pushy. I know they're going to spill all your stories. But they love the heck out of you. It's obvious. You are lucky to have them. And I feel lucky that you're sharing them with me for Christmas."

If the words hadn't shocked her enough, Cash leaned forward and pressed a whisper of a kiss on her forehead. Before she could find her voice, he opened the door and pulled her inside to find her family.

CHAPTER TEN

"No. I didn't bring my uniform tonight," Cash said to Nana, not for the first time. Her eyes twinkled at him and he couldn't help the chuckle that escaped.

Ripley looked like she wanted to crawl under her chair again. *Sorry,* she mouthed to him, giving him pleading eyes across the dinner table.

He shook his head. He couldn't get annoyed by Nana. Sweet wasn't the right word for her, but it was hard for him not to be charmed. He could put up with her feistiness and the repeated questions. As a bonus, whenever Nana did something to embarrass her, Ripley's cheeks turned pink. Cash loved that look on her. With her family constantly jibing her, it had been a constant look throughout dinner.

Nana winked at Cash, as though sharing a secret, then bent closer to him. "I'm not really senile, you know. Perk of being an old bag. I can repeat myself a million times and people just assume I don't realize. You can get away with everything when you're older. File that away for later."

His chuckle became a laugh. "I guess this means you really do want to see me in my uniform?"

Her eyes lit up. "Young man, you're a very good listener."

Cash could see Ripley leaning forward across the table, trying to catch their conversation without even being subtle about it. He turned to whisper in Nana's ear. "Maybe for Christmas morning? Though something tells me you aren't on Santa's nice list."

"Oh, I'm most definitely on the naughty list. Eighty-seven years running." Nana's laugh sounded deep and throaty, like in her younger days she had spent a lot of time smoking. Patting him on the shoulder, she spoke to Ripley, who was watching the two of them nervously. "This is a good man you found yourself. Don't let him go."

He grinned at Ripley, who smiled back, then flashed ten fingers at him. Ten smiles. She told him after the grocery store that she had been counting each one. Cash wondered if he would get to a point soon when she'd stop counting, because smiling would be more normal. Honestly, until she mentioned it, he hadn't realized how seldom he smiled. Ripley made it easy.

It was moments like these where the reality of what they were doing suddenly hit him square in the chest. In a normal relationship, you wouldn't spend Christmas with the other person's family after one date. But nothing about this was normal. Not from the start, not now. Even if it felt somehow completely right. Cash fit in with her family. He liked them. Even Ripley's brothers, despite their drive to humiliate her as much as possible. They all seemed to wholeheartedly approve of Cash too.

Could this be real?

Cash had shoved feelings so far down inside himself for years that in these moments of clarity, he had to take a moment to get his bearings. The strange thing was, this lighter, more relaxed Cash felt more like him than the closed-off man he'd been for the past two years. Being around Ripley made him feel like he was peeling back the layers to find himself again. The idea both thrilled and terrified him.

Ripley smiled, reaching between the empty dishes to find his hand. Instantly, he shoved the questions back where they belonged. Which was far from this table filled with noise and laughter and light. But most importantly, Ripley.

"Oh, Cash!" Seth, the younger of Ripley's older brothers, slung his arm around Gillian's shoulders, a gleam in his eyes. "Did we tell you about Ripley's first boyfriend?"

"Seth! You promised!" Now, even the tips of her ears were red. She pulled her hand away from Cash to cover her face, and he immediately missed the contact.

"But I didn't pinky swear," Seth said. Apparently, pinky swears were hot currency in the Johnson family, and as binding as a blood oath.

"This story isn't so bad," Chris said. He was wrangling the aptly nicknamed Tommy Terror, who was driving a toy car through the bowl of mashed potatoes. No one but Cash seemed bothered by this. It definitely curbed his appetite for seconds. "It could be worse. He could tell the one about—"

"Stop!" Ripley held up her hands. "Please. I was not this bad when you guys brought home dates."

Her sisters-in-law exchanged glances, then said in unison, "Yes you were!"

"Worse!" Seth said. "Cash, do not let Ripley fool you. She may seem sweet, but the girl is vicious. Utterly. Especially when it comes to playing poker or dominoes."

"Poker, huh?"

She sniffed and lifted her chin. "We play for candy, not money."

He didn't care what they played for. Poker had just been added to his ever-growing mental agenda of things he wanted to do with her. He hoped it was a Christmas tradition, but no one had mentioned it.

"Poker for candy sounds delicious." Cash turned to Seth. "Tell me more about this viciousness. I think I need to be fully prepared for what I've gotten into."

Laughter filled the room. Even Ripley, who was now shoving Seth, giggled. When she turned to glare at him, Cash reached across the messy table and took her hand again. Seth launched into the story about her first date, where the guy told her to dress up. Apparently, she thought that meant in costume.

"Rather than change, when the guy showed up in a dress shirt and nice pants, Ripley held her head high and went out to dinner with him dressed as Where's Waldo."

"I made a choice to fully commit and see it through," Ripley said.

Cash could see a glimpse of that determination in the set of her jaw now as she defended herself. He tried to picture her years younger, going on a date in costume. What did Waldo wear? He could only picture a red and white striped hat—or was it a shirt?—and a walking stick.

"Tell me you had a walking stick?"

"She borrowed my cane," Nana said. "I never use the thing."

The table roared with laughter, Cash included. He couldn't actually remember the last time he laughed so hard. Ripley shook her head at them all, but even she had a smile. More importantly, she didn't let go of Cash's hand.

He glanced up and down the table at the warm, laughing faces. They were teasing, but the laughter held no malice. It was playful and fun. The kind of ribbing that came from a place of love. He had no doubt now that Ripley would give it right back. The ache of longing that had been growing in the center of his chest fanned out like a flame. He wanted this.

Despite a few years of pushing away the thought of love and marriage—for very valid reasons—the past few hours had stirred awake his desire for a family around a table. Teasing, laughter, inside jokes. And a woman whose hand he could hold right next to the almost-melted stick of butter and the green bean casserole.

He didn't just want this with someone. Cash wanted this with Ripley.

It was way too much and way too soon. Especially given that two days ago, he would have said that he never wanted this. A few days ago, Ripley was simply a woman he'd given a ticket. One who got under his skin.

She was definitely under his skin now. But he needed to slow down. The change was too fast. He knew that. Yet he wasn't having much luck putting on the brakes. Especially not when her thumb began tracing the back of his hand. Heat traveled from her touch up his arm, not stopping until his whole body felt like it might ignite.

"Cash, is this different from how your family celebrates Christmas Eve?" Ripley's mother leaned her elbows on the table and rested her head in her hands, waiting for his answer.

All that heat turned to ice.

In his conversations with Ripley, he'd managed to say as little as possible about his family. On the spot, with everyone staring, he couldn't brush the question aside as easily. He should have been more prepared though. It would have helped him not have such a visceral physical reaction.

Ripley squeezed his fingers, and he met her eyes. Her look was encouraging and soft. There was no pressure there, only understanding and curiosity. But he could see beneath that, a steady warmth and support. As though whatever he said here wouldn't make or break things between them.

His eyes dropped to the table as Ripley continued making small circles on the back of his hand with her thumb.

"My mom left when I was nine," Cash said. "It was just me and my dad. So things were a lot quieter." He really didn't want them asking for more details, so he did his best to smile and turned the conversation. "Thank you for letting me join you this year. The food was amazing and I'm really looking forward to tomorrow."

Ripley's mother glanced at Cash with concern. "Are you not joining us for the Christmas Eve service? Tell me we're going to a Christmas Eve service, Ripley."

Her face paled. "Oh, I hadn't realized—"

"You hadn't realized that this is something we do every year? And you're the one who works as a planner. Get out the Yellow Pages, Walter. Find a church. Any church."

In all the teasing, Cash hadn't seen Ripley actually look upset. But now, her eyes darted as though she was going through mental lists. Her free hand was clenched around her water glass. He hated seeing her stress.

"We can go to my church," Cash said. The table quieted. "There are a few services tonight. We've missed the early family service, but there's one at seven thirty and then a midnight service that starts at eleven."

Cash glanced at his watch, then at Tommy Terror, who had moved to the living area and now looked like he was trying to unstuff the throw pillows.

"Good man," Ripley's dad said. He got up from the table and stretched. "Better take my nap so I can be ready for the eleven o'clock."

Cash didn't hide the surprise on his face. Guess they were

all night owls. Was that true for Ripley as well? One more detail to find out. He wanted to learn all the small parts that made up this gorgeous, fun, amazing woman with the wild and loud family.

Jackson, Jenna, Mercer, and Beau would be at the later service. Other than Jackson, none of them knew about Ripley. They were in for a shock when he showed up tonight with her and her whole family. Maybe it would be better to drop that bomb now rather than at Jackson's dinner. He felt a tiny flicker of nervousness, but it was quickly eclipsed by excitement. He couldn't wait for them to see Ripley on his arm. Ripley seemed to think there might be some awkwardness with Emily after the wedding, but she and Jimmy were in Richmond until the day after Christmas.

"Why don't you two lovebirds take a walk?" Nana said. "It'll be hard to find time for kissing with all these people around."

"Nana!" Ripley pulled her hand away from Cash to fan her hot cheeks. Cash felt heat creeping up his neck, but not from embarrassment. The idea of kissing Ripley had that heat returning to his body. He pulled at his collar.

"Kissing! Gross!" Tommy yelled from the couch, which he was now using as a trampoline. Cash really hoped Jackson would be understanding about whatever state the house was in at the end of her family's visit.

Nana squeezed Cash's arm and waggled her eyebrows at him. "Well, if you're not going to kiss him ..."

Cash pushed his chair out from the table as Ripley's family roared with laughter.

"How about a walk on the beach? Kissing optional." He winked, and Ripley's cheeks went from pink to bright red. Even her neck and chest flushed. Her gaze snapped to his. Cash swore that underneath the embarrassment, there was a different kind of heat in her eyes. Did the kissing talk have the same effect on her as it did on him?

There were whistles and catcalls as Ripley hooked her arm through Cash's. They headed for the stairs, but she turned back before they started down.

"You are all horrible and I hate you."

"You know you love us!" Chris shouted. "Have fun making out!"

"Don't do anything I wouldn't do!" her mother called.

"Do anything you want!" Nana yelled. "Just remember you'll have to sit in church in a few hours."

As they walked down the three flights to the bottom level of the house, Ripley sighed and rested her head on Cash's shoulder. "Still glad you agreed to this?"

He grinned. "I wouldn't have wanted to miss a moment of this. Trust me."

CHAPTER ELEVEN

R ipley rubbed her hands together, then shoved them down into the pockets of her coat. The breeze coming off the ocean was unforgiving. But despite the fact that every exposed bit of her skin was freezing, being away from her family for a few minutes was worth any cost. And walking next to Cash, their shoulders brushing with every step, had her nerves firing on all cylinders.

"It's not fair that the beach is cold at Christmas," Ripley said. "When I moved here, I assumed it would be warmer. I hate winter. Like, really hate it."

Hate might not have been a strong enough word. Ripley had realized the last year of college that her struggle through winter was a touch of seasonal depression. She'd invested in a sun lamp, which helped nominally, and also indulged in small doses at a tanning salon.

That wasn't something doctors recommended, but she heard about it on a message board for women struggling with seasonal depression. The coconut smell of tanning lotion, the sweat-inducing heat, and the brightness beyond her protective goggles did wonders. She only did five to ten minutes at a time, once or twice a month, and slathered herself in sunscreen. Hopefully, her skin wouldn't be too damaged. But the way it lifted her spirits made it totally worth it. There was only one tanning salon on the island and she'd purchased a monthly membership in early November.

"You'd really hate Boone. This is nothing. Winter in the mountains is pretty dismal. Unless you love that kind of thing. Which I don't."

She gave an involuntary shiver. "Charlottesville was close enough. The rest of the year was great. But not winter. Do you get a lot of snow in Boone? I'm sure it's beautiful."

"Beautiful, yes. But kind of a cold beauty."

That was a lovely description. Cash really did have a way with words. He was almost poetic at times.

"Do you like living here? On Island, as they say." Cash didn't remove his hands from his pockets, but she could almost hear the air quotes when he said *On Island.*

Ripley smiled. "They, huh? You don't see yourself as an On Islander yet?"

"Yes and no. The community has been very welcoming. I love it here, but I can't say I feel like I fully belong. Or that it feels like my home. Yet. You?"

Ripley was quiet for a moment, working through the words before uttering them. "I'm not sure that I even halfway belong. I've actually thought about moving home when my lease is up. I haven't really made many friends."

"That surprises me."

She felt like there was a compliment in there somewhere, but he didn't elaborate. "I work a lot. I'm pretty close with my co-workers. But I tend to be a little set in my ways. Getting out of my comfort zone can be hard. I probably haven't made as much effort as I should. Like with going to church. Thanks for letting us come with you tonight. I can't believe I forgot. That's a huge part of our family tradition."

"Of course. It's no big deal. You've had a lot on your mind this week. No pressure, but if you'd like to go with me again, you're welcome anytime. That's where I met all my friends. They're some of the best I've ever had."

"I did visit once," she said, chewing her lip.

"I don't remember seeing you. And I think I would have remembered." He gave her a sideways glance that sent her heart racing.

"I came in a little late and sat in the back. Left as soon as it was over."

"Huh. You don't strike me as shy," Cash said.

Ripley shrugged. "I'm not exactly shy. But there's something about walking into church alone, sitting alone, and having no one talk to you. Doesn't really inspire confidence, I guess."

"Doesn't sound like you made it too easy for people to talk to you. Coming late, leaving quickly."

He was right, of course. She hadn't really given it a chance. "We'll see how tonight goes."

Cash chuckled. "You won't be able to hide in the back with your family."

"Definitely not. We're more likely to get kicked out." A harsh wind picked up, colder and more blustery than the ocean breeze. Ripley took her hands from her pockets again and blew on her icy fingers.

Cash grabbed both of her hands in his and spun her to a stop. Immediately, she felt ten degrees warmer. And not just because his hands were big enough to fully envelop hers. No, the heat was more of an internal flush that started in her chest every time Cash touched her or gave her one of those smiles that made her jittery.

Like the one he flashed her now, his teeth gleaming in the moonlight. "If you wanted to hold my hand, you could've just asked," he said, his tone light.

"Oh, I didn't mean—I was just …"

Cash made like he was going to drop her hands. "You don't want me to hold your hands?"

"It's fine," she said.

"Just fine?" His eyes twinkled. When he started to pull his hands away again, she grabbed them.

"Frustrating man," Ripley said, narrowing her eyes. "You need me to say it?"

Cash shrugged, a smile playing on his lips. Ripley realized that she had lost count somewhere during dinner.

"Communication seems like a good start to a relationship," he said.

Relationship. He said relationship. Is he thinking of this like that too?

Her heart sprinted wildly. She had to swallow twice before she could find her voice again. She tried to keep it light so he wouldn't suspect the inner freak-out she was having.

"Cash, would you mind holding my hands? They're freezing," she said in an overly sweet voice.

His grin widened. "Is that the only reason you want to hold my hands?"

Rolling her eyes, Ripley snatched her hands back and started off down the beach. It was hard to storm away in the dark while walking in sand, so she only got a few feet before Cash caught her. His strong arms wrapped around her waist, and he pulled her tight against his chest. Ripley struggled a little but not enough that he would let her go. That was the last thing she wanted.

With a sigh, she stopped fighting and leaned back against

him. His hands found hers and covered them, even as his arms stayed tight around her. "Much better," she said. "You've been holding out on me. You're like a furnace."

"Are you saying I'm hot, Ripley?" His beard brushed over the shell of her ear, making her shiver. He started to pull away. "Aw, you're shivering. We can go in."

"No!" She wouldn't let him remove his arms and settled back against his chest. "I need a breather from my family. And I guess the company isn't too terrible. If you don't mind."

"Mind? I could get used to this."

"Are you flirting with me, Officer?"

"It's perfectly legal when I'm not on the clock."

Ripley felt like someone should pinch her. His flirty words, his warm chest against her back, his lips close to her ear—it all felt like the kind of thing she'd dreamed about. And yet, even a few days ago, she never would have imagined it.

"Well, then, I won't try to stop you. Or give you a ticket. Unlike some people I know."

"You were speeding," he said. "And I've already said I'm sorry."

"I know."

Cash rested his chin on her shoulder, and she could smell him over the salty ocean breeze. It couldn't be aftershave, since he had a beard. She wondered if it was cologne, body wash, or just something distinctly Cash. Despite the bitter wind and the cold that still seeped into her, Ripley didn't want this moment to end.

Was it really this easy to slip into a relationship? Could she trust in something that felt so good, so perfect, so fast? Especially when it all hinged on a lie she still hadn't cleared up with her family.

"Do you have any nicknames?" he asked.

"What?"

"I was just thinking about your name. Ripley. Doesn't lend itself to nicknames so much. Rip sounds too ... violent. And Lee doesn't quite suit you."

"I guess I really haven't had any."

"Where'd the name come from? Is it a family name?"

She snorted. "Hardly. In addition to my brothers, I have a long list of male cousins on both sides. I was the first girl in years. My parents thought it was cute." She waited for him to get the joke. He stared blankly at her and she sighed. "As in, Ripley's Believe It or Not? Believe it or not, we had a girl! They thought that was hilarious."

"It fits you though. I like it. And makes perfect sense given your family."

Ripley's chest tightened. "They're a lot to handle. I'm sorry. Do you have any brothers or sisters? I don't know how we got away from dinner last night without me knowing that."

It felt as though an iron box came down around Cash. Every bit of his body stiffened. And then his arms slipped away from her waist and he stepped back. She turned to face him, wishing she hadn't asked the question. But it was such a simple question. What was so bad about his family that he completely shut down about them?

"I was raised as an only child," he said. In the darkness, Ripley couldn't make out his eyes, but she could read the stiffness in his body. Tension practically radiated off him. "We should head back."

Ripley's disappointment came in waves. She felt like she had gotten beyond Cash's outer surface. But one wrong question and he closed another door and flipped a deadbolt. The disappointment eased slightly when he took her hand, lacing their fingers together. It surprised her, as she half-expected him to storm back to the house in front of her.

Ripley was thankful for the ocean's roar and the whistling wind. It kept the silence between them from being too overwhelming, too conspicuous. Maybe he wouldn't realize that she was hurt at being shut out.

What did she expect? That he would spill all of his secrets to her? Share whatever hurts he'd faced in his past? They barely knew each other.

Yet, after an evening spent with her family, things felt deeper between them. More real. And Ripley had been totally vulnerable. Cash knew her now in ways that she wouldn't have necessarily wanted him to. He'd heard embarrassing stories from her childhood and he had whispered secrets with Nana. With her family there, she had no choice but to let Cash all the way in. Even though his hard exterior had melted into smiles and teasing, she still felt like she didn't know him. Because he kept holding back.

She felt laid bare, and he kept closing the door on her. It was a simple question, but she knew that his answer about being an only child wasn't the full story.

"I'm sorry." She almost missed his whisper over the roar of the ocean. "I'm not used to opening up. It's something I'm working on. It may not be fast."

"That's okay. As long as you know that I'm here."

He pressed a quick kiss to her head. "Thank you."

As they made their way back to Jackson's, Ripley leaned further into the warm solid protectiveness of Cash's shoulder. She promised herself that she wouldn't push him, as much as it was hard to be missing key details about his life. She would give him as much time as he needed. But even as she made that vow, the busy part of her brain was already wondering how she could help fix whatever it was.

CHAPTER TWELVE

As Ripley drove them to church, her family following in a small caravan, Cash smiled at the snowman dancing away on the dashboard. Her car was immaculate and had no personal touches except for the snowman. It had been an impulse buy. Maybe it was small, but it was the first gift he had bought for a woman in years. He loved that she had put it right in the center of her dashboard where she would see it every time she drove.

She yawned.

"You okay?" he asked.

"I'll get a second wind." She waved a dismissive hand. "I do every year. If I happen to fall asleep in the service, poke me before I start snoring."

"You snore?"

Her eyes went wide, and she shot him a quick glance. "No. It was just a joke."

They met up with her family in the parking lot. Cash could feel Ripley's nerves in the way she clutched his arm as they walked into the building. Her family had the subtlety of a traveling circus, drawing immediate attention. Ushers by the sanctuary doors handed them small white candles with a paper cuff to catch the wax.

"This might be bad," Ripley said, eyeing the candle, then Tommy. He was already chewing on a candle while his mother tried to pry it from his hands. "Tommy and open flames don't mix."

"Good thing Beau's a firefighter," Cash said. "We should be fine. Just in case. But I do think you're right to be concerned."

"Based on your vast experience of my family?"

He nudged her shoulder. "Yep. I'm ready for my Johnson family pop quiz. Anytime."

Cash caught sight of Beau as they moved toward the sanctuary doors. He and Mercer were up on the stage, tuning their guitars. Tommy broke away from his mother, who looked exhausted, and made a run for the stage, where some decorative candles were already lit.

"Fire!" Tommy said. "I like fire!"

"Get back here, Tommy! Chris! Can you catch him? You're faster than me." Mel groaned in frustration as her husband chased after Tommy. The little boy had almost made it to the front of the church where candles were lit when Beau stepped down from the stage and blocked him.

Beau knelt down, and Tommy's fixation on the flames moved quickly to the guitar strapped to Beau's chest. Beau simply smiled as Tommy pulled the strings and put his probably sticky hands all over the glossy wood. Beau's eyes met Cash's and then flicked to Ripley with surprise. A grin broke out over his face. A few days ago, Cash might have felt embarrassed and exposed by the attention, but right now, he felt a swell of pride being with Ripley.

"We should probably sit near the back. Just in case

Tommy ..." They both watched as Chris managed to scoop him up, carrying him away from Beau kicking and screaming.

"Say no more," Cash said. He turned and held an arm out to the empty row near the back of the room. "Is this okay?"

"Only if I get to sit next to you, handsome," Nana said. Ripley's parents supported her, but she shook them off and reached for Ripley and Cash instead. The rest of her family filed into the row, Tommy practically being restrained by his dad. Cash found himself sitting with Nana on one side and Ripley on the other.

Jackson strode over with a brilliant grin as they settled in. "You must be the Johnsons," he said.

Ripley stood to shake Jackson's hand. "Thanks again. Everything is perfect. A vast improvement over my tiny apartment."

"Glad to hear it. Let me know if you need anything."

"You might need new throw pillows," Cash muttered. Jackson only chuckled.

"This is the billionaire who owns the beach mansion?" Nana practically shouted. A few people turned in the rows ahead of them.

"Nana!" Ripley whisper-shouted.

Cash put his arm around her and pulled her back down to the seat beside him, tucking her into his side. This made Jackson grin even wider.

"Jackson Wells, ma'am. It's a pleasure to meet you." Jackson took her hand and pressed a quick kiss to Nana's knuckles.

"My my." Nana fanned herself with the paper program for the service. "This island must have something in the water to breed such handsome men. Know any octogenarians looking for love? Or a good time?"

Cash wished he could have taken a photograph of Jackson's face. His mouth opened and closed several times before he could respond. Even Ripley giggled. Jackson shot them both a look but quickly recovered and smiled at Nana. "Not at the moment, but I'll keep my eyes out."

Ripley's father stood and shuffled down to shake Jackson's hand, but before he could say more than a quick thanks, the music started. Other than Nana, who waved them off, they all stood for the first song.

"Where's Jenna?" Cash asked before Jackson moved away to his row.

"Not feeling well. She went to bed early." With a pat to Cash's shoulder, Jackson moved away to a row closer to the front.

"You'll like Jenna," Cash whispered to Ripley. "Mercer too. I even think you and Emily will be friends."

"I hope so."

They turned toward the front and joined in the traditional carols, led by Mercer's rich voice. Cash could hardly carry a tune and mouthed the words, but Ripley had a clear, high voice that matched well with Mercer's as she picked out a harmony to "Away in a Manger." Cash put his arm around her shoulders, leaning closer to hear her better.

The Christmas Eve service reminded Cash a little too much of home. After his mother left, he and his father had become Christmas and Easter churchgoers. But still, the memory hit him deep. He had to choke down the bitterness rising in his throat. His own family had fallen apart. Yet here he was with Ripley's family, who brought him in immediately.

Was his father attending a church service tonight with his new family?

As though sensing his conflict, when they sat down after a few songs, Ripley pressed closer to him, her scent rising up to fill his nose. *I'm making new memories,* Cash thought. *I don't need to let the old ones ruin these.*

Without so much as a second thought, he pressed a kiss to Ripley's temple. She gazed up at him with a smile so gorgeous that he struggled to catch his breath. Panic shot through him, and as the pastor led them in prayer, Cash lifted up his own silent one.

Lord, what am I doing? I didn't want to meet someone else. I didn't want to let myself feel again. Was this a mistake? I don't want to get hurt. I don't want to hurt her.

His scattered thoughts began to settle as he prayed, even though he didn't have any answers or any kind of sudden assurance to ease his worries. When the pastor spoke of angels telling Zechariah and Mary not to be afraid, Cash felt that same promise being extended to him.

Pastor David's voice was warm and sure. "Jesus told them, 'I have told you these things so that in me you may have peace.' In him. Not in our financial security or our love. Not in our families or the gifts under the tree. Not our homes, not our jobs, not our identity. Our peace is in him. Perfectly guarded. Fully trustworthy. Do you know what else he promised? He promised trouble. We will have trouble in our lives. But we will always have his peace."

That was just the assurance Cash needed. It might not be easy. Things with Ripley could crash and burn. But he still had peace. Jackson's words came back to him: If it was part of God's plan, Cash couldn't screw it up.

Ripley squeezed his hand. They exchanged a glance that felt much too weighty for how long they'd known each other. Definitely too emotionally charged for church. Tommy interrupted the moment, appearing at Cash's feet suddenly and climbed up into his lap. Down the aisle, Chris whisperhissed, "Tommy! Tommy!"

Cash waved Chris off and let Tommy settle in on him and Ripley. Within two minutes, he was asleep across both of their laps. Just like Nana, whose soft snores had both Cash and Ripley fighting off giggles.

"Based on genetics, I'm going to go ahead and hazard a guess that you do snore," he whispered to Ripley.

She jabbed a finger into his ribs and Cash tried not to stir Tommy awake as he flinched. When the lights went down, Tommy was still sleeping. Ushers lit their white candles from the Christ candle in the advent wreath at the front of the church. Right as they lit Ripley's candle, Tommy wiggled to life and made a grab for it. Hot wax fell on Cash, who tried to keep it—and the flame—from Tommy.

Cash could not remember wrestling a more slippery suspect. By the time Chris made it down the aisle and plucked him from Cash's lap, his pants were dotted with wax. He even had some on his wrist that he suspected would leave him a little bit hairless when he pulled it off.

"Guess I should have just blown this out," Ripley said quietly as she lit Cash's candle from her own. Nana slept through it all. "Sorry about your pants. Feel free to send me a bill. I'll pass it right on to Chris. I have a feeling it will just be the start of a long line of bills he'll get because of Tommy."

"Nope. This is all on you. At any time, you could have blown out that candle, instead of wrestling with a toddler and destroying my pants. I'll pass on the bill to *you* in the morning."

"You just try," Ripley said.

Cash loved teasing Ripley, and he loved whispering to her even more. It meant he got to lean close, feeling the warmth rising from her skin and her intoxicating scent. She smelled like tropical beaches and summertime.

"I'll do more than try," he said.

She shivered at his words, and as they raised their candles, standing to close out a chorus of "Silent Night" with only voices, Cash heard his watch beep the midnight. He leaned close once more until his lips were close to Ripley's cheek.

"Merry Christmas, beautiful."

Cash realized as the words left his mouth that he'd just given Ripley a nickname. It couldn't have suited her more.

CHAPTER THIRTEEN

Ripley woke Christmas morning to the sound of Tommy shouting, "Is Christmas! Is Christmas!"

His small but mighty footsteps thundered on the stairs above her. She could hear Chris shouting at him to be quiet. Smiling, she stretched in the queen-sized bed, which was much larger than her bed at home. More comfortable too. She could get used to this: a large, lavish home right on the beach. Too bad she'd have to move back to her cramped apartment in a few days.

Her belly felt aflutter with the excitement of Christmas morning, except her thoughts weren't on gifts under the tree. They were on three words Cash had whispered in her ear the night before: *Merry Christmas, beautiful.*

Cash thought she was beautiful. Her lips stretched into a wide smile. When she looked at herself in the adjoining bathroom mirror, she even looked different somehow, as though Cash's words played out on her skin. Her cheeks were flushed, her eyes brighter. Her hair seemed shinier. Even with her sleepy eyes and mussed hair, she looked like a woman in love.

Love. Where had that word come from? It shocked her, but that didn't make it a less apt description. Not that she *was* in love—it had to be way too soon for that—but she simply had that look about her.

"Ripley! Roll yourself out of bed! Tommy wants to start opening gifts." Her mother's shout carried all the way down the flights of stairs to her room at the bottom.

"Be right up!" she called.

Ripley didn't bother changing out of her pajamas but did put on a bra. She didn't remember what time Cash had said he was coming. Checking her phone, she found a message from him, sent about ten minutes before.

Cash: Morning, beautiful. Not sure what time y'all get up, but I'm on my way. Figured Tommy might be an early alarm clock. Need anything?

Ripley made it up the last set of stairs, her fingers paused over the keys. Before she could change her mind, she bit her lip and sent a two-word response: *Just you.*

Too much? It was hard to know anymore. Fighting this felt like fighting gravity. Whether she wanted to or not, Ripley was already going down.

While watching Tommy open presents, Ripley started questioning her text. Especially since Cash didn't respond. Or show up. She'd never been to his apartment, but he said it wasn't far. The island was only so big. Did she scare him off? Shouldn't he have been there by now?

Her mother seemed to read her thoughts. "Where's Cash? Did he tell you what time he's coming?"

"I'm not sure," Ripley said. "Soon, I think." *I hope.*

"You're in charge of the cinnamon rolls."

Rolling out the cinnamon roll dough and creaming butter and brown sugar was a great distraction. Her mother had been making cinnamon rolls for Christmas morning since Ripley was a girl. They were enormous and so rich that she only made them once a year. Her thoughts kept running back to Cash, listening for the door downstairs to open as she put the finished pan of cinnamon rolls in the oven.

When she heard a door close and his feet on the stairs, relief flooded through her. She ran down the steps to meet him on the second level. Her brothers, jerks that they were, catcalled and whistled as she ran. Cash rounded the top of the stairs on the second floor, a tray of coffees in hand. Ripley stopped on the landing, blinking up at his handsome face and grinning like a fool. The smile dropped when she took in his uniform.

"Oh no—do you have to work?"

He grinned. "I promised Nana."

Ripley covered her face and made a strangled noise. "Oh no. She's going to ogle you."

"It's fine. And my Christmas sweater is in this bag, so I'll have that too. Why aren't you in yours?"

"I try to delay as long as possible until Mom forces me," Ripley said. She giggled. "I can't believe you're wearing your uniform for Nana."

He shrugged, and she swore that she saw his cheeks darken slightly. "What can I say, I'm a sucker for older ladies."

"Do I have something to be worried about?"

"My only worry is that you're about to spill the coffee."

Ripley had been so distracted by his uniform that she had forgotten about the coffees he carried. "You brought coffee! What's open on Christmas Day?"

"This place I like is open three hundred sixty-five days a year. It's down at the southern end of the island, which is why it took me so long." His eyes shifted up the stairs where voices carried. He leaned a little closer to her. "I didn't bring enough for everyone. Do you think that's okay?"

Ripley gripped his shoulder for balance and stood on tiptoes to kiss his cheek. She loved—no, *liked*—the way his beard tickled her lips. "You couldn't supply us all with coffee. There are too many of us. Mom has a pot brewing upstairs. So, who gets lucky?" She eyed the three coffees in the carry-out tray.

"Oh, these are all for me."

She narrowed her eyes. "I'd shove you, but I might spill the coffee. But as soon as you set it down, you're fair game, Officer."

Cash grinned. "I covered the most important bases: you, me, and Nana. I got her decaf."

She was touched that he remembered Nana saying how she loved coffee, but the caffeine was hard on her heart. Ripley tugged Cash's elbow and began pulling him upstairs. "You're brilliant. Now get up here before they start—"

"Lovebirds! Stop making out and get up here!" Seth shouted.

Ripley groaned, but she was still smiling. Even her brothers couldn't dampen her spirits this morning. "Too late."

When they reached the top of the stairs, Nana caught sight of Cash and began to laugh. "Well, what a Christmas surprise! Put that coffee down and do a nice, slow spin for me, will you?"

"Nana!" Ripley shouted, just as her father yelled, "Ma!"

Her brothers laughed hysterically, and their wives tried to look like they weren't looking as Cash stood in front of the fireplace and slowly turned. Ripley covered her eyes, but looked between her fingers, giggling the whole time. She told herself it was to be sure Nana wouldn't try to stuff dollar bills in his pants or something.

He didn't swivel his hips or anything as he spun, but he didn't need to. The man filled out his uniform well. But Ripley liked him almost as much in his ugly Christmas sweater and flannel pajamas when he changed a few minutes later. She suspected it didn't matter what Cash wore. He was far too good looking.

As the morning went on, Ripley felt love bloom like a hot flower in her chest. It was that sense of Christmas magic and having her family all together. The scent of cinnamon rolls baking and fresh coffee. The crinkle of wrapping paper and soft Christmas music playing underneath the laughter.

But a big part of the warmth in her chest was having Cash beside her. Sharing her family with him felt like a much bigger step than she'd anticipated when they agreed to this.

She couldn't remember a happier Christmas morning. Even Tommy calmed down some, which was shocking considering the massive pile of toys and candy he'd eaten. He channeled all that energy into building a small Lego set that Cash had brought for him.

"I didn't think he was old enough for that kind of set," Chris said, straightening out the instruction booklet for Tommy.

"Maybe you've got an engineer on your hands," Cash said. He made his way back over to the couch, where Ripley sat with her coffee in hand and her legs tucked underneath her.

"You didn't need to bring gifts," Ripley told him. "No one expected that."

"It's not much," Cash said. "I loved doing it."

His gifts might not have been big, but they were thoughtful. Warm socks for Nana, a subscription to a gardening magazine for her mother, a crime novel for her father, and gift cards to restaurants for her brothers and sisters-in-law. Her family, in turn, had showered him with gift cards to places like Home Depot and the big sports and outdoors place. Nana, oddly, had given him a leather-bound journal. It seemed like a very personal gift and more serious than what Ripley would have imagined.

He hadn't given her anything yet, other than a Santa hat that matched the one he wore. She got the sense he was waiting. Which made her feel terrible because she hadn't thought to get him anything. A major oversight on her part. Between that and forgetting about the Christmas Eve service, Ripley felt like a total failure. Things like that never escaped her attention. Maybe it was the whole thing with Cash throwing her off. Or the New Year's event, which was drawing closer and suddenly had all kinds of issues. She had to work in the morning but could get him something before the dinner at Jackson's. Before she forgot again, she made a note in her phone.

"What's the rule with keeping the sweaters on?" Cash asked, leaning closer. "I'm getting pretty hot."

Yes, you are. Ripley cleared her throat. "You can take it off," she said. Looking relieved, Cash began to lift the hem. It jingled as he did. "But you'll face the wrath of my mother."

Sighing, he let the hem fall back down. Ripley couldn't help the grin on her face. Her whole family looked like a tacky Christmas store had thrown up on them, and she loved it. It was the kind of silly tradition she hoped to carry on with her own family in the future. This year, her sweater was white and had real lights threaded all over. It even played music. After a few rounds of "Joy to the World," her mom let her slip the switch to turn off both the lights and the music.

Ripley crossed the room to the balcony and cracked the doors to let a little cool air in. Cash nodded his thanks. With the oven baking cinnamon rolls, a fire going in the gas fireplace, and the Christmas sweaters, the room had definitely gotten a little stuffy. Outside, the day was sunny but cold. The sound of the ocean filtering in mixed with the Christmas carols someone's phone played and the ripping of paper.

By the time the cinnamon rolls and breakfast casserole came out of the oven and they finished eating, it was almost noon. Cash scraped the last bit of cinnamon filling and a piece of pecan from his plate. Ripley watched as he drew the fork up to his lips. If she had to make a Christmas wish, it would definitely involve those. She realized that Nana was watching her as she watched Cash.

Maybe she didn't notice. Nana winked. *Nope. She definitely noticed.*

Embarrassed at being caught, Ripley began stacking plates and carried them over to the sink. Cash invaded her space. "Move over, beautiful."

"You're not washing dishes," she said, not budging from her spot. "I've got this."

"It's Christmas. Let me help."

Ripley flicked water at him. "It's Christmas," she said. "No."

"Don't be a scrooge," he said, sticking his hand under the faucet and flicking water back at her.

Ripley squealed. "Fine. Fine. But be careful of the sweater. It's very important to me. I wouldn't want to get something on it."

"Clearly. I'm not sure how you wash a sweater that's electronic."

"Dry-clean only," she said. "And if you're billing me for the wax on your pants, you better believe I'm giving you my Christmas sweater dry-cleaning bill."

Ripley loved the way their heated first conversations had melted into something softer, but still with spark. Outside of her family, she hardly talked to anyone this way.

His phone buzzed a few times while they were washing plates, loudly enough for Ripley to hear over the sound of the running water. "Need to get that?"

He dried his hands and pulled the phone out of his pocket. Without really meaning to, Ripley glanced down, seeing that it was a text from his dad, wishing him a Merry Christmas. There was more, but that's all she could see before he tucked the phone away again.

"No one important," he said.

His words chilled her. No matter how embarrassing her family could be, she loved them. This was exactly the way she would have wanted to spend the holidays. Even with all the teasing.

What could be so bad about his father that Cash wouldn't talk about him and screened his calls on Christmas day?

It seemed so unlike the man she'd gotten to know the past few days. She had invited Cash right into the fray and he didn't miss a beat. He put up with Nana's inappropriate flirtations and all the teasing from her parents and brothers. He was open and gracious. Even sweet. He'd gotten them all presents and hardly knew them.

Yet he was dodging his dad's calls and had been for days. The thought hurt her heart. But maybe being with her family would help open him up to deal with the clearly unresolved issues with his own.

Ripley and Cash washed dishes for a few minutes with the sounds of her family creating a happy cacophony in the background. It had been nine months since Ripley had been with all of them together. She'd had an event on Thanksgiving Day, so she hadn't gone home. Too much time had passed, she decided. And having Cash beside her somehow made her feel like she fit in with them more.

"Thanks for spending the day with us," Ripley said. "It's been really nice to have you."

"I hope it helped take the pressure off."

That's right—taking the pressure off. That was the whole reason Ripley had pretended she had a boyfriend in the first place. Maybe he hadn't meant it that way, but his comment suddenly made her wonder if this whole thing might be a charade.

The words sent a shock through her system. Was that how he saw things? As simply an arrangement that benefitted them both? A way to take the pressure off? Did he simply feel sorry for her—the woman her own mother had said might turn into a cat lady? Insecurity washed over her like a tidal wave.

Logic tried to fight off the onslaught, but she couldn't seem to hold back the worries. Was he simply playing a part? Had she read him all wrong?

"I've got to go to the bathroom," Ripley said, practically bolting away from Cash. She made it down the stairs to her room before a single tear fell.

Once she had closed the door behind her, she stood with her back against it, trying to talk some truth into herself. Crying over one comment was ridiculous.

He said he liked you. He called you beautiful. He put on his uniform for Nana. He fits with your family.

He fits with you.

The truth was, this realization terrified Ripley. If it was real, she was terrified, just as much as she was if it were all what it started out as: a lie that got away from her. Could something real truly come from that?

A knock sounded on the door at her back.

"Ripley?" Cash's low voice curled around her chest. She pressed a hand to her heart.

"Yes?"

"Is everything okay?"

Not remotely. If all this ended in a few days' time, Ripley didn't know if she could recover. She could already imagine the cold, empty place that Cash currently occupied. And if it were real? If it were real, she was surely falling too hard, too far, too fast. At the least, she needed to get control of her heart. At the most, she needed to guard it and understand that he had not once said that he saw this arrangement going past this week.

Trying to compose herself, Ripley opened the door. Her eyes moved from Cash's questioning glance to the wrapped gift in his hands. A gift? That brought the tears right back.

"I didn't get you anything yet," she whispered, not able to take her eyes off the box with a silver ribbon that looked to have been tied professionally. Okay, so she'd panicked for nothing. "When did you have time?"

"You don't have to get me anything," Cash said. "I like giving gifts. That's one of my favorite things to do. And it's been a long time since I've had anyone to shop for."

Again, Ripley found her thoughts snagging on his past. Why didn't he have anyone to shop for? What happened to his family? Why wouldn't he tell her about them? Maybe she simply needed to push a little. Or give him the invitation to share.

"First though, I wanted to say that this is more than simply something to get your parents off your back. I didn't mean it that way."

Ripley smiled down at the carpet. "Was I that obvious when I bolted?"

Cash chuckled. "If you were a cartoon character, you would've had smoke trailing behind you when you ran."

He lifted a hand from the gift box to touch her cheek. She looked up and met his blue eyes. In the light of day, up close, she could see flecks of gray mixed with the blue. It only made them look more like the ocean. She wanted to dive into them and lose herself in their depths. Ripley felt desire surge in her to know this man and to uncover the secrets he held behind his eyes. She wanted to earn his trust.

Instead of taking the gift, Ripley reached up and covered his hand where it rested on her cheek. "I want to say something too. I don't want to pry. If you don't want to tell me about your family, you don't have to. But I'm here. If you want to talk. You told me that my family is nothing to be embarrassed about, so maybe yours isn't either."

"Thank you." His voice was low and rough. He pressed the gift into her hands. "Are you going to open it?"

She smiled, determined not to be upset that he hadn't taken her invitation to open up. She needed to be patient with him. Even if that wasn't her strong suit. "Okay." She untied the ribbon and opened the box. Nestled on the tissue paper, she found a delicate chain with a thin silver feather charm. It was nothing she ever would have thought to buy for herself. She loved it instantly.

"Wow. It's beautiful."

"It will match your sweater perfectly," he said, his eyes twinkling.

"Put it on?"

The moment felt oddly intimate as Ripley turned, lifting her hair away from her neck. Cash fumbled with the clasp for a moment and then she felt the slight weight of it and the cool metal against her skin. Cash's fingertips grazed over her neck, then he took her by the shoulders, turning her to face him.

Ripley let her hair fall over her shoulders. He tucked a piece behind her ear. "I love it. Thank you, Cash."

One minute, she was staring into his wild ocean eyes, and the next, his lips brushed over hers. It was a whisper of a kiss, a soft caress. When he pulled back, it took a moment for Ripley's world to right itself again. Her eyes fluttered open.

"Merry Christmas, beautiful," he said, smiling.

What number smile was that?

Ripley found that she had completely lost count.

CHAPTER FOURTEEN

"I want all the details," Phyllis said. "Even the dirty ones."

"You and my nana need to get together, Phyllis. But there are no dirty details." Ripley had so much work to do. They all did. The catering company had several servers come down with the flu, and they had warned her they would be short-staffed. A few other last-minute issues had reared their heads, yet Amber and Phyllis were gathered around her desk. Probably because Deondra had a meeting at the location.

"So, he hasn't kissed you yet?" Amber asked, her eyebrows shooting up.

Ripley's blush answered that question. "Just a tiny one. It barely counted."

Phyllis cackled. Amber had a hazy look on her face. "And how was this tiny kiss?" she pressed.

Ripley didn't know how to put it into words. Not the quick brush of his lips, which felt like something much deeper and much more serious. It felt like, in that moment, something had been sealed between them. A promise of things to come.

"It was good," she said.

"Good," Amber repeated. "Nope. Not buying it."

Sighing, Ripley set down her pen. "Fine. Then we all need to get back to work. Okay? It was amazing. He's amazing. I really like him."

"Where's the but? I hear it in your voice," Phyllis said.

"It's just so ... fast. A few days ago, I barely knew him. Now? He's spent time with my family. I feel like it's moved really quickly. But we're barely more than strangers." She thought of his ignored phone calls from his dad. The way he kept his guard up.

"Strangers who kiss," Amber said with a smile.

"Sometimes love happens that fast," Phyllis said.

Ripley looked horrified. "Oh no. I didn't say love."

Phyllis winked. "Sure, sure. Whatever you say. I'll let you work now. Just send me a wedding invitation." The older woman made her way back to her desk.

Amber sized Ripley up with a look. "Maybe it's not love—yet—but you are smitten."

"That's a good word for it. I'm a mess. And I don't remember the last time I felt this way about a guy. Any guy." Ripley paused. "You don't think it's too quick to feel this way? I mean, we were arguing in here just the other day."

"Fighting is just another way passion rises to the surface. Don't question it. Just enjoy the ride."

Amber went back to her desk, but her words lingered. Ripley wasn't good at enjoying the ride. Never had been. She thought long and hard about the ride, made lists, and finally, color-coded plans and spreadsheets. She had already thought way too hard about future plans with Cash. Not because she was one of those obsessive girls who latched on to a guy right away. It was simply how her brain worked. She had to think of best- and worst-case scenarios. This wasn't something she was proud of about herself or openly shared. People didn't tend to understand.

Right now though, she needed to stop worrying about Cash and get working on the real-life worst-case scenario of their catering company being under-staffed because of the flu. When Deondra called the office an hour later, she hadn't thought about Cash once. But she had found another company with servers to supplement the losses.

Deondra's normally cheerful voice sounded tight. "Can you and Amber come down here? Phyllis can lock up and work from home if she wants. But I wanted to get your eyes on the space."

"Sure," Ripley said. "Is there an issue?" They'd made the reservation a year ago. New Year's Eve bookings filled up quickly. A few months ago, all four of them walked through the space, finalizing plans.

Deondra sighed. "Since we were last here, they did some renovations. It will impact everything from the band to where we set up tables. Really, everything needs an overhaul."

Tension built in Ripley's shoulders. Her fingers were already itching to take notes. "Shouldn't they have let you know? I mean, that's usually standard in contracts. Right?"

"Someone dropped the ball. What they've done falls within the contract, but it's quite inconvenient. I think having you and Amber walk the space might help. My brain is fried."

"Understandable. We'll be there soon."

"Great. Oh, and before I forget—did you ask Cash to come? How are things going?"

Dang her co-workers for being so involved with her sudden love life. Then again, Cash ensured that by coming to her office twice. "They've been good. I haven't asked him yet."

"Don't forget," Deondra said, a smile in her voice. "I'd hate for you to miss out on a New Year's kiss."

Just the thought of another had Ripley's stomach doing gymnastics. She'd been hoping for more, but so far, just the one. She drove separately, mostly so she didn't have to answer any more of Amber's questions about Cash. On the one hand, he was all she could think about and she would have loved a sounding board. But it was all so fresh and new. She didn't have enough emotional distance to be objective about her feelings. And with Amber being single, she wouldn't go on and on. She knew just how that felt. The happiness for someone else mixed with the ache of longing.

As she drove, the dancing snowman kept catching her eye on the dashboard. Even though the day had been cloudy, he'd picked up enough sun to keep his hips moving. He had on a scarf and sunglasses, a forever smile fixed on his face. "That's some easy life you've got there, buddy."

She wished for a little bit of that easy life when they walked into the Sandover Event Center. The permit taped to the glass doors was a bad start.

"Uh oh," Amber said as they walked into the event hall. There were painting tarps and ladders and power tools lying around the lobby. Part of the lush rug had been pulled away from the floor, exposing the concrete. "This is ... different."

"It's a nightmare." Ripley felt sick looking at the space. She could visibly see the hours in the coming days, sucked away into whatever extra work this project would now take. How would this get done in time? What were they thinking starting something like this before an event?

Deondra met them at the door to the main ballroom,

walking with brusque strides. Her mouth was a firm line. "Thanks for coming. You can already see the issues."

"They didn't tell you they planned to make massive changes?" Ripley asked. "Or think about how this would impact us?"

"Apparently not," Deondra said. "There's a new manager and—well, a whole lot more I could say about it. Wires were crossed, mistakes were made. Too late to fix those." She waved a hand and then smiled. "This is what we have to work with. They've assured me that the work will be done, and the space will be ready. But come inside to see how the design changes will impact everything. Then we can update our plans and contact vendors as needed. We've got this."

That was one thing she appreciated about Deondra. No matter what bumps in the road—or, in this case, cavernous sinkholes—she simply did her best to adjust and move on. Ripley pulled a notebook out of her purse and began jotting down notes as they walked.

Though this would undoubtedly mean a lot more work between now and New Year's, she was somewhat thankful. Without something like this to sink her teeth into, she had a feeling she would be obsessing over Cash. In only a few days, she already felt the tug of her thoughts toward him. What was he doing now? How was his patrol? Was he safe? Was he thinking about her? So, yeah. This would mean massive work, but a good way to keep her from becoming a little obsessive.

When they hit a break and she had four pages of notes written, Ripley ducked into an alcove and sent him a text.

Ripley: You might already have New Year's plans, but if not, want to be my date?
Ripley: I'm technically working, so I might be a little spotty.

But it's a black-tie gala at the Sandover Convention Center. Should be fun.

His response came back almost instantly.

Cash: I wouldn't want to be anywhere else.
Cash: I'll pick you up at 6. Can't wait to see you.

Who would have guessed that underneath the grumpy cop, such a sweet man existed? In two hours, she would get to see him again. Not that she was counting. Smiling, she tucked her phone back into her purse and caught up with Deondra and Amber, who were headed out to the parking lot.

"You're glowing," Deondra said. "Which is surprising, given the amount of extra work we're going to have now."

"Cash is coming with me on New Year's."

Amber pulled her into a hug. "I'm so happy for you."

"You don't mind?" Ripley asked. "I don't want to leave you in the lurch."

"Please," Amber said. "I'll be fine. I'm really happy for you. Just promise me one thing."

"Anything."

"If he has any friends who aren't taken ..."

"All yours," Ripley said with a smile.

"I'll see you both bright and early tomorrow," Deondra said. "I hate to do it, but plan on living in the office this week."

CHAPTER FIFTEEN

"Whatever you're doing, don't stop." Emily hopped up onto the counter next to the sink, drying a platter with one of Jackson's dish towels.

"I'm sorry?" Ripley stiffened. That had been her reaction to Emily all night. She hoped it would get easier, but their interactions had been fairly awkward. After all the tension between them at the wedding, Ripley didn't think Emily would want her crashing their tight-knit little group. She'd done her best to stick near Cash. Which wasn't hard, considering he hardly went a moment without holding her hand or touching her in some way.

But now the men reclined around the table, while Ripley, Mercer, and Emily washed dishes. Not—as Emily vehemently pointed out—because it was a woman's job, but because the guys made dinner. Now, Emily nodded toward the table where Cash, Jimmy, Beau, and Jackson were talking and laughing. When Cash caught Ripley looking, he winked, his smile widening.

"Cash," Emily said. "Whatever you're doing, don't stop. I've never seen Cash smile like that."

"I've never seen him smile. Period," Mercer said.

"Oh, really?" It shouldn't have been that surprising to Ripley, but she had assumed that maybe with his friends he had been more open and easygoing. Like he was right now. "This isn't normal for him?"

"This is all you," Mercer said. She handed another rinsed dish to Emily to dry. Beau's fiancée couldn't be more different from Emily on the outside, though the two were best friends. Jenna, Jackson's wife, had a headache and was lying down before they went down to the beach for the bonfire. She had been friendly, but it was clear to Ripley that she hadn't been feeling well.

"When we met, I thought he hated me," Ripley said, smiling.

"He's like that with everyone. You've somehow managed to crack the iron barrier around Cash. You deserve a medal," Emily said. "How'd you do it?"

Ripley loaded a plate in the dishwasher and leaned against the island to face Emily and Mercer. "He gave me a ticket."

Emily threw her head back and laughed. "Best start to a relationship ever."

"Oh, that's not all," Ripley said. "Then he took my phone from me and my mom thought he was my boyfriend."

"Wait—why would she think that?" Mercer asked, her brow furrowed.

"I might have told my mother that I had a boyfriend. It was just a ploy to get her to stop hounding me about being single."

Emily laughed again. "I like you. I wasn't sure. But between Cash and this? Yep. You're golden. I mean, wow.

Cash has always been pretty stiff. He's like a different person."

"That's not fair," Mercer said. "I've seen his good side. Even if it wasn't a particularly jovial side."

"Exactly. He's a good guy. But did he ever smile or look happy like this?" Emily countered. "My point is that I think he's smiled more tonight than I've seen him smile since I moved to Sandover."

Mercer glanced over at the table. "Yeah. I guess you're right. He was kind, but not ... happy."

Ripley felt warmth ripple through her limbs. Did she really have that big of an impact on Cash? The insecure part of her that still didn't trust in whatever was building between them wanted reassurance. Things had been good between them the past few days, but there was still the whole awkward start to this whole thing. The fake boyfriend aspect.

It was hard to shake the very real fear that their rocky start based on a lie and a misunderstanding could result in heartbreak. That maybe they weren't on the same page about all this. It also still worried her that he had no relationship with his family. It was a red flag for sure. But he had been so amazing with her family.

"Sorry, Ripley," Emily said. "You're stuck with us. We aren't going back to grumpy Cash. You'll just have to stay. You don't mind, do you?"

Mind? Ripley hadn't realized how lonely she had been at Sandover until this week. Not just the time with Cash. But having her family around, going to church, and now being around a group of friends—it only revealed the emptiness that had become her life.

"I guess I can live with that. I'm a little surprised you seem excited. I mean, after the wedding, I wasn't sure."

Ripley didn't like confrontation, but she'd prefer getting this out in the open. Then she wouldn't be constantly circling the drain in her thoughts. She felt it hanging between them all night.

Mercer gave a small laugh and Emily elbowed her. "Sorry," Mercer said. "But you were totally a bridezilla. Someone has to say it."

"I was not!" Emily said. She flicked the dish towel at Mercer, who backed up and used her hands as a shield. "I was super low-key about the whole thing. Totally chill. The opposite of my mother."

Ripley managed to keep her mouth from falling open, but Mercer met her eyes and then shook her head.

"You may not have been your mom, but you were anything but chill," Mercer said. "You were opinionated about everything. Just not the same things as your mom. Ripley did an amazing job and I'm shocked she didn't lose it on you. Or quit."

Emily glanced at Ripley. "Tell her, Ripley. I wasn't a bridezilla."

Behind her, Mercer nodded vehemently and mouthed *Yes, she was!* Ripley turned away from the sink to face Emily. "I don't use that term. But you were a ... challenging client."

She wanted to hold her breath as Emily's jaw dropped. Maybe being so honest with her after one dinner was too much. Emily blinked and looked to Mercer, who nodded.

After what seemed like too long, Emily shook her head. "Dang. Here I was thinking I was all actualized and self-aware. I didn't want the fancy things my parents did, so I thought that meant I was easy. I was difficult?"

"You were," Mercer said. "But we still love you."

Emily turned to Ripley and stuck out her hand. "I'm sorry

138

for being a problem client. Truly. Though I still think my mom was worse."

"She was."

Emily grinned. "Friends?"

Ripley bit her lip to hold back her smile. "Friends. Don't worry about it though. Weddings are amazing, but the planning and details are incredibly stressful. For everyone."

"You can say that again," Emily said, turning back to the counter. They fell back into their routine of washing and drying. Ripley scrubbed, handed a plate to Mercer for rinsing, and Emily dried. After Ripley's nerves about the evening, and about the conversation they just had, the routine action was soothing.

Ripley glanced at Emily. "You and Jimmy seem really happy. I think I'm staying in the house where you guys rekindled your relationship."

Emily grabbed her arm, her eyes wide. "The balcony house?"

"That's the one."

"Jax!" Emily turned back to the table, hands on her hips. "You're letting Cash's girlfriend stay in the house I almost died in? Have you no respect?"

Ripley only half listened to Jackson's response about codes and updates and permits. Instead, she was watching Cash's reaction to Emily's words. His face cracked open in a beautiful smile aimed right at Ripley. She couldn't hold back her own wide smile.

So, he didn't mind thinking of her as his girlfriend. Good thing. Because Ripley didn't just not mind. She liked it. A lot.

An hour later, seven of them huddled around a bonfire out on the beach in front of Jackson's place. The crackle of the fire and the steady crash of the waves formed a perfect soundtrack to the end of the evening. Mercer passed out wire hangers that had been straightened for marshmallow roasting, while Emily fussed at Jimmy for eating chocolate straight out of the wrapper.

Jenna still hadn't emerged from her bedroom, and as they began roasting marshmallows and sharing memories of Bohn's, Ripley could tell that Jackson missed her being by his side. He stood with one hand stuffed into this jacket pocket, letting his marshmallow burn into a black husk. The other couples were paired off, snuggling together for warmth against the cold breeze. Even Cash had given up roasting marshmallows to wind his arms around Ripley's waist. The warmth of his chest against her back spread through her. She didn't want to move again. Ever.

"This okay?" Cash asked.

Ripley couldn't help the shudder that went through her at the feel of his lips so close to her ear. She wanted him to kiss her again, but he hadn't. Was there a reason? Despite the way he had opened up, Cash still had so many mysteries under the surface. Though Ripley hadn't dated much, the relationships had always seemed so much clearer. The expectations and understanding. A guy asked you out; you went out. It worked, or it didn't. With Cash, one minute she felt secure and the next, he was pulling away and making her question everything.

He said he liked me. He spent the last forty-eight hours with the circus that is my family. Emily and Mercer said I make him smile. He likes me.

Doesn't he?

Cash must have felt her shudder and his arms tightened around her. "You're cold. We can go in if you want."

"I'm fine. We're staying."

Even if it hadn't been for the amazing way it felt to be in his arms, Ripley wouldn't have left. The night was supposed to be about Jackson and saying farewell to Bohn's. They'd met at the store before dinner and done a walk-through of the empty space. Ripley didn't tell anyone that she shopped at Harris Teeter, and Cash didn't spill her secret, thankfully.

Bohn's was a different kind of store. Ripley had only been in it once and only noticed the prices. Tonight, she had followed along, listening to stories that they shared. About how Emily injured her toe on frozen ground beef while trying to sneak up on Jimmy. How Jackson gave Mercer a job, which led to her staying at Sandover and meeting Beau. Jenna had run into Jackson there when she moved back and apparently insulted him, thinking he was a bag boy, not the owner.

"How was I supposed to know that the high school playboy became a billionaire?" Jenna had asked, giggling as Jackson kissed her neck.

Ripley had felt like an outsider until Cash realized she was trailing them. He had snagged her hand and made her walk with him.

But since then, they had almost forgotten about Bohn's. It hadn't been mentioned, but it seemed that a little melancholy washed over them all.

Jenna walked out from the beach house then, a blanket wrapped around her shoulders. Jackson's face lit up and he gave her a sloppy, happy kiss on the mouth.

"Champagne time!" Emily said, pulling a bottle out from a bag that lay at her feet.

"Champagne and s'mores?" Beau asked.

"Champagne and everything," Emily said. "Sparkling cider for Jackson, of course."

Jackson didn't drink. What was the story there? The longer the night went on, the more Ripley wanted to know these people and their lives. Cash most of all. But she liked the added bonus of being friends with his friends. They were good people. Even Emily, who had surprised her.

But if things didn't work out ... If this all ended after Christmas and the things they needed dates for ...

Ripley swallowed hard. She wanted to trust in the strength of Cash's arms around her waist. In the solid feel of his chest, warm and supportive. But fear never seemed to stop creeping into her thoughts.

"Cider for me too," Jenna said.

There was a beat of silence. The men might not get the significance there, but as Ripley glanced at Emily and Mercer, she realized that it was, in fact, a big deal.

Emily squealed. "Are you serious? How long?"

Mercer grinned and moved closer for a hug. Jimmy and Beau looked confused, and Jackson's grin could have overshadowed the moon.

"What's going on?" Cash whispered.

"I think Jenna's pregnant," Ripley said.

She couldn't see Cash's face for his reaction but felt him tense as the nostalgic goodbye party turned into a celebration. Ripley dropped her roasting stick as Emily pressed a plastic flute of champagne in her hand. She offered one to Cash as well.

"No, thanks," Cash said.

Emily moved on with only an eye roll by way of comment. Ripley felt the shift in Cash. What did this news mean to him? Was she imagining his reaction? She couldn't have been. As the rest of the group moved into toasting and laughing, she suddenly felt more on the outside than she had when she was following them in the store. Cash was pulling away.

But why?

She never found out the reason. After the celebration wound down, Jenna went back upstairs, saying she still felt terrible. Now that everyone understood why, they all went their separate ways. No one else seemed to notice Cash's sullen mood. Maybe because that was his normal.

Ripley had been hoping for a goodnight kiss, but Cash didn't get out of the car. Not even to open her door. He rolled down the window and called out to her. "Goodnight, Ripley."

"Are you sure you're okay?"

"Just fine," Cash said.

"Okay. I've got to work a lot in the next few days. I'll be pretty busy."

"That's fine." She expected him to promise a phone call or a text. But he had rolled up his window and started backing away before Ripley had put her first foot on the steps. He was anything but fine. Would he ever tell her why?

Or maybe—and Ripley really didn't want to think about this—now that their Christmas week was over, their relationship was too.

CHAPTER SIXTEEN

I'm pregnant, Cash.

As he drove his cruiser the next day, his eyes darted from the road to the rows of homes and the slope of dunes on his left. The sun felt too bright. Sounds were too loud. Just catching a glimpse of the ocean, dark gray and angry, helped drown out the voice in his head. Not the radio. Not his own shouts. Not covering his ears. Only the wildness in the waves helped silence her voice in his head.

I'm pregnant.

He pulled into the lot of a beach access, this one at the other end of the island from Jackson's house. He couldn't risk seeing anyone he knew today. Walking up the worn wooden steps to the beach access, Cash let the scent of the ocean fill his lungs. He leaned his hip on the rail and breathed deep. The sea and salt in the air soothed him, but the sand stung his cheeks as the rough wind tore by him. The weather had taken a decidedly nasty turn this morning. Just like his mood.

Pregnant.

Closing his eyes, Cash tried to pray, but couldn't clear his mind enough, even with the ocean. This was usually his happy place. It's why he ended up at Sandover almost two years ago when he left Boone. As he drove across North Carolina with only a few bags he'd tossed into his car, Cash had tried to erase the last conversation he'd had from his mind.

Clearly, it didn't work.

"I'm pregnant, Cash."

He had stared at Olivia across the kitchen table in his father's house. Even as they had sat down to talk, he had been thinking that it was high time for him to move out. For years, he had stayed. He didn't need a shrink to tell him that it was partly because his mother left. He didn't want to be anything like her, so he wouldn't leave his father. The two of them were now more like a couple of bachelors in the big house that still seemed empty from his mother's absence.

What did Olivia just say?

"I don't understand. You're ... pregnant?"

Before she dropped her gaze to the mug of tea in her hands, the look she gave him confirmed her statement. Her hands shook.

It wasn't his baby. It couldn't have been. The physical part of their relationship consisted of a lot of restraint and hours of stolen kisses. Holding hands. Holding her in his arms. They were waiting for marriage. It was something they decided on together, that mattered to both of them.

But she hadn't waited with someone else.

Someone else.

She was cheating on him. And now was pregnant. The facts made their way through his consciousness one by one.

"Whose is it?"

He winced at his words. Cash never thought he'd use the

term *it* for a child. A baby. While he feared that he might not be a great husband or father, he longed to be a daddy. To provide for his own child what he always wished he had growing up. A tiny he or she with ten fingers and ten toes. Not a bundle of cells. Not an it.

The words tasted wrong in his mouth. Everything about the moment felt wrong.

While he waited for an answer, he looked at Olivia. Really looked at her. Nothing had changed about her shoulder length blonde hair and big brown eyes. But those three words made him see her completely differently. Olivia wasn't the woman he thought she was.

He didn't know her at all.

"Whose?" His voice was rougher this time. He didn't like the edge in it, the threat of violence that it held beneath it. Her head snapped up, mouth open. He had never spoken like this before to her. It was a voice reserved for his job. Dealing with criminals and law-breakers. Not his girlfriend. Ex. His ex-girlfriend. Because no matter what her answer was, this was over.

"Mine."

It had been like something from a movie. Everything slowed down. Cash even turned around in slow motion to see his father standing in the doorway. Not standing, leaning. As though he couldn't stand up under the weight of his confession.

Cash hadn't asked for any more details, though his mind surged with questions. Here, in the house? How long? When did it start? How could they? He stood from the table and walked away from them both.

He didn't speak again. Wouldn't answer when his father called out to him. He simply packed a few bags and left. For good.

It hadn't even been so much about his feelings for Olivia or the distinct shame and humiliation of having her cheat. No, it was the gut-wrenching understanding that his own father had been the other man. They destroyed the only family Cash had left. The man who had done his very best to raise Cash alone had slept with his girlfriend?

It was unbelievable. Yet, there it was.

It didn't take Cash long to get over Olivia. But he would never get over the betrayal. He would never be a part of his family again. How could he? Now, his ex-girlfriend was his stepmother and mom to his half brother. Twenty-four years between them.

That had been a few days before Christmas, two years and three days ago. This was the first year he hadn't spent the week of Christmas dealing with the still-raw emotions of it all.

Because this week, he'd been with Ripley. He had her whole family around him, helping pull him up out of the darkness that usually consumed him around this time of year. And he'd had Ripley, with her coconut scent, her soft skin, and her easy smiles. The witty banter between them. For the first time in two years, Cash hadn't been wearing the past around his neck like a chain. The pain and betrayal that stayed with him and reared up every year around Christmas had eased.

Until Jenna's announcement, which made the memories slam into him with the violence of a hurricane.

I'm pregnant, Cash.

He hadn't seen Jenna's announcement coming, and the onslaught of memories took him down to his knees. Not literally; he continued standing there on the beach with Ripley, his arms around her waist, her hair tickling his neck, while his world shrank into a tight ball of pain.

He knew Ripley could tell something was wrong. Part of him thought to tell her. To confess for the first time exactly how much of a mess his family was. How much of a mess *he* was.

In the end, Cash had driven away, knowing that he was shutting Ripley out. She had been nothing but open with him, inviting him into her family. But he still couldn't talk about it. He didn't know if he ever could.

If he wanted to move forward with Ripley, he would have to. He knew that. He knew that she would understand. It's not like Cash had done anything wrong. But it felt like a confession nonetheless. His dad and Olivia's shameful secret had somehow become his own.

Cash had to calm himself down. His breathing was erratic, his heart rate all over the place. Physically and emotionally, he ached. Every part of him. Leaning his elbows on the wooden railing, he let his face sink into his palms. The cold wind coming off the ocean bit into his skin, but he didn't even mind.

His phone buzzed, and he pulled it out of his pocket, halfway expecting another message from his father or Olivia. They had been relentless the past few weeks. Didn't they know that pushing him only made him go farther away?

But the message was from Ripley.

Ripley: My family is headed out soon. I know you're working this morning, but if you wanted to come say goodbye, you've got about an hour. I know Nana would love to see you in your uniform again.

Ripley: Selfishly, so would I. ;)

Cash couldn't help but smile, though her words made guilt twist in his gut. Even after he pushed her away, she kept inviting him in. He didn't deserve it. But he wanted to be that kind of man.

Realization washed over him. It wasn't enough to simply tell her about his family. He needed to deal with the bitterness and anger that he'd been holding on to for two years. Whether he had a relationship with his father moving forward or not, Cash had to forgive him. Forgive *them*. He had to let go.

At first, the voice telling Cash that he needed to forgive them had been loud. The longer he ignored God's prompting, the quieter that voice became. Today it seemed to be screaming at him, rivaling the sound of the wind.

Cash needed to forgive his father and Olivia.

The thought took his breath away. He straightened, his hands shaking. He clutched the railing, feeling the bite of the rough wood on his palms.

He couldn't do it. Even if it meant living with this pain buried deep in his chest. Even if it meant being miserable. It was just too hard. Too much to forgive.

But could he move on in his life while holding onto his bitterness? Could he build a relationship with Ripley without dealing with his past?

"You doing okay, Officer?"

Cash hadn't even heard the man walking up from the beach with his golden retriever on a leash. The man's gray hair whipped around his face in the wind and he carried a tennis ball in his free hand. The dog stopped to smell Cash's shoes. He knelt and scratched it behind the ears. Other than Tony, Mercer's dog, he didn't get a chance to be around them much. He would have loved to do a K-9 program, but Sandover didn't have one.

"Just taking a moment to enjoy the view," Cash said.

The man nodded. "I always like the ocean just before a

storm. We're due this afternoon." His dog pressed his wet nose into Cash's palm, urging him to keep up the scratching. "Don't feel like you need to keep petting him. James won't stop begging once you start."

"James?" Cash's hand stilled on the dog's neck until the wet nose nudged him again.

The man chuckled. "My wife thinks it's funny giving dogs human names. We've had Barry, Charles, and Michael before James."

Cash stood. He wasn't taken aback that the dog had a person's name. James was the name of his half brother. The one he'd never met. Because God hadn't already been shouting loud enough at him. He had to send a dog named James too.

"I know it's a day late but Merry Christmas!" The man and his dog walked past Cash and headed toward the parking lot. He watched as they got into a battered Suburban and drove away.

Cash still felt the turmoil seething in his chest. He knew what God was telling him to do but didn't know if he could do it. Would he ever have peace if he didn't?

He climbed into his cruiser. Ripley's family would be leaving soon. Though he hardly felt like he was in the right frame of mind to make polite conversation, he had to go. Ready or not, he needed to say goodbye.

CHAPTER SEVENTEEN

R elief moved through Ripley when Cash pulled up in
front of the house. After the way he closed down the
night before, she wasn't sure that he would come. Which
certainly would have broken Nana's heart. Her own too, if
she was being honest. Cash hadn't just gotten under her skin
this week. He had climbed inside and carved out a living
space for himself. How had that happened? She didn't even
realize until he suddenly pulled back the night before, leaving
a cavernous empty space beneath her ribs.

Ripley rolled the last wheeled bag to the back of the van
as Cash climbed out of the car, looking broody and handsome. His expression was hard to read behind his aviator
sunglasses. But he smiled and kissed Nana on the cheek,
helping Ripley's father walk her to the van.

Maybe everything would be fine. But an unease settled in
her gut. Especially when he didn't come over to say hello.
Ripley watched him saying goodbye to her family. Her heart
felt tight when he shook her father's hand, then did the
whole hug with a lot of back-slapping with her brothers. The

sisters-in-law and her mom got kisses on the cheek. Tommy Terror clung to his legs until Mel pulled him off.

"He's a good one," her mother whispered in her ear as she hugged Ripley. "Hold on to him."

She could only smile, blinking back the tears. Somehow, she didn't think that holding on to Cash was something she had the power to do. He finally came to stand next to her after everyone had loaded up into their cars.

"Hey," she said.

"Hi." He gave her a small smile but didn't move to touch her in any way. She'd gotten so used to him holding her hand or putting an arm around her that the distance between them made her ache.

What had changed the night before?

Her brothers drove off, honking and waving. Only her parents remained, the minivan idling in the driveway. She wished they would all go, even Cash, so she could fall apart in private. Nana rolled down her window.

"I'm thinking about relocating," Nana called. "The views are much better, and the men are more handsome. Ripley, do you need a roommate? Or do you have other plans?" She winked at Cash, who took a small step away from Ripley.

Her cheeks burned. The normal teasing felt like too much today. She did her best to fake a smile. "I can always use a roommate, Nana. But I get to hold the remote."

"Never mind, then. Cash, it was lovely to meet you. Take good care of our girl."

"Will do," Cash said.

"Don't be a stranger!" her mother called as they backed away.

Ripley waved until they turned the corner. Her dad honked the horn once and then they were gone. Wiping her eyes, she glanced at Cash. What she wanted was to lean into his chest and let him wrap her in his arms. But a gulf had opened up between them. She didn't know why, and she didn't know how to close it.

"Thanks for coming. I know my family really enjoyed you being here."

So did I.

Ripley couldn't force herself to say the words. It felt too much like putting herself out there while he was pulling back. She'd already given so much of herself.

"This week has been really nice," Cash said.

Nice. The word rolled around in her mind. It was a friend word. A breakup word. Tears threatened to resurface but she swallowed them down. She waited for him to finalize it.

Instead, he gave her shoulder a quick squeeze. "I've got to get back to work. You said you'll be pretty tied up until New Year's?"

When he let go of her shoulder, Ripley hated how much she missed the physical contact. "Basically, I'm going to eat, sleep, and breathe work. Our event has turned into a disaster."

Ripley wanted to ask if he still planned to be her date for New Year's. Get it all on the table. Deal with the sting of disappointment. If he was pulling away, she'd prefer it like a Band-Aid, just ripping it right off. A quick bite of pain. Though the pain of losing Cash would be anything but quick.

The part of her that couldn't bear to see things end won out, and she stayed silent. Did it make her naive to live in denial a bit longer?

A call came over his CB and Cash started off. "That's my cue," he said. "I'll talk to you soon?"

"Sure," Ripley said. As he climbed into his car, the rain started, falling in sheets that stung her cheeks and hands. By the time she made it up the steps and inside the door, she was drenched. And Cash was gone.

"Do you want to talk?" Amber hovered over Ripley's desk.

She set her pen down on the desk and rubbed her temples. "Is it that obvious?"

"Pretty much. Or, I'm observant. And I observed a big change in you this week."

Ripley thought that she'd hid things well over the past two days. The issues with the event space made it easy. All four of them had been working nonstop, with Deondra going back and forth to the space, making sure the renovation was on time. But even work couldn't fully distract her from the fact that she hadn't talked to Cash since her family left.

Sighing, Ripley glanced around, surprised to see that Phyllis and Deondra were gone. How had she not noticed? She didn't even know what time it was.

"How about we grab dinner?" Amber asked. "You haven't eaten all day. I noticed that too."

"I guess I'm not going to make any more progress tonight."

"Nope. So, come on. Let's go out. Even if you don't want to talk, we need a break. This event is killing us."

Ripley nodded, closing her laptop and packing up her things. Twenty minutes later, she sat in a booth across from Amber, twisting her hands.

"Do I need to put out a hit on a certain hot cop?"

Ripley snorted and Amber smiled, flashing her dimples. "Nothing like that."

"So, he didn't break your heart? Because you seem

deflated. Just a few days ago, you were floating. What happened?"

"I don't actually know. And that's the problem." As the food came, Ripley told Amber about her week with Cash, ending with the way he shut down after the night at Jackson's. "Something happened. He shut down. I just don't know why. I was thinking that maybe he always had an expiration date on this. Like, he just wanted to do the dating thing this week. And only this week."

Amber took a sip of her milkshake. "Is that what he said when he took you to dinner?"

Ripley tried to replay the conversation. It made her heart hurt thinking about counting his smiles and the snowman that still danced on her windshield. "I'm not sure. I thought he was asking me to date him, but he specifically mentioned the time with my family and the dinner with Jackson."

"But he said yes to the New Year's gala?"

"Yes. We haven't talked about it since. Or talked at all. I guess he's still coming? I'm scared to ask."

Amber leaned forward. "Let's go back to the night at Jackson's. Things were fine until suddenly they weren't?"

"Yep. The girls were telling me they hadn't seen him smile so much. When we were out by the bonfire, he had his arms around me."

"And then Jenna announced that she was pregnant?"

"Yes. Which may be a secret for now. So keep that quiet."

"Of course." Amber looked thoughtful. "What if it's a baby thing? Or, if not a baby thing, a future thing."

Ripley let this idea turn over in her mind. "You think he got gun-shy? Thinking about commitment? Like the pregnancy talk made him think too much about the future or something?"

"That or a secret-baby thing." Amber laughed, then

waved a hand. "Joking. My best guess is that things suddenly felt serious. You said it moved quickly, right?" Ripley nodded, and Amber continued. "A lot of guys have issues with commitment. From what I know, Cash hasn't dated since he's moved here. And believe me, there's been interest. He's a catch. But he's been the uncatchable catch until you. Maybe he just got scared."

Maybe. But Ripley suspected there was something more. His reluctance to talk about his past. The screened phone calls from his dad. He fit seamlessly into her family yet acted like his didn't exist. There was something bigger. She just didn't know what. And he didn't seem likely to tell her.

Amber grabbed her hand over the table, her eyes wide. "You know what you need?"

Ripley had no idea. Her relationship experience had clearly failed her. "What?"

"A killer dress for New Year's Eve."

Ripley tried to pull free from Amber's grip but couldn't. "Yeah, right."

"We'll go shopping. I'm great at that kind of thing."

"I have a dress," Ripley said.

"You may have a dress, but you need a *dress*. Trust me on this. I'll be your PSA."

"PSA?"

"Personal shopping assistant," Amber said with an exaggerated eye roll.

"Right. And with our insane schedule, when exactly are we going shopping for this *dress*?"

Amber finally dropped Ripley's hand and pulled out her phone. She typed something into it while Ripley finished her water, trying to get her bearings. How could she tell Amber that a dress wasn't going to fix what was wrong with Cash?

"Done," Amber said. "I talked to Deondra. We're going

shopping tomorrow afternoon. Before you argue, don't worry about work. I've got it all figured out."

Ripley stared down at her plate, where half her chicken sandwich sat, uneaten. "I don't know how a dress is going to make a difference."

"It won't," Amber said. Ripley's gaze shot up to her face. "The most gorgeous dress can't fix deeper issues. And if a guy only wanted to work things out because of how amazing you look, he's not worth your time."

"Then, why can't I wear the black dress I planned to wear?"

"Because the dress I help you pick out will open the door to the conversation you need to have. It won't close a deal. But it will start the conversation."

Blowing out a breath, Ripley leaned back in her chair. "Fine. But what about the actual conversation? What do I say to him?"

"I mean, you're asking the single girl." Amber shrugged. "Hear him out. If he's scared of commitment, maybe time will fix that. Maybe it won't. But if you really like him, don't give up so easily. Promise me that. Promise."

Amber held out her pinky. Ripley couldn't help but smile. "Did you know that pinky swearing is my family's thing?"

"Nope. But smart family. Now promise me."

Ripley held out her pinky finger but pulled back from Amber. "What exactly am I promising?"

"You're promising not to give up too soon. You're promising that if you really like him, you'll put yourself out there. Even if you get hurt. You'll try. I mean, if you think he's worth it."

Ripley hooked her pinky around Amber's. Cash was definitely worth it. The big question was whether or not he thought that she was worth it. She had much less hope of that.

But she didn't back out of pinky swears. Silly as it might seem, that was something her family had been doing for years, and Ripley took it seriously.

Cash may not want to keep things going. But Ripley wouldn't give up. Not without trying.

On the drive home, Ripley couldn't stop staring at the snowman dancing on her dashboard. Its smile mocked her. When she got caught at the never-ending light just before her apartment, Ripley rolled down the window, pulled the snowman from the dash, and tossed him out on the side of the road.

At the next intersection she made a U-turn and went back to pick up the broken pieces. Ripley couldn't decide if it was because she was sentimental or simply didn't want to litter.

CHAPTER EIGHTEEN

C ash walked through the doors, pulling at the sleeves of his tux jacket. He'd had to borrow one from Jackson for this event. Though they were close enough in size and build, it wasn't an exact fit. Kind of like this whole event, which was far too posh for him. It was a charity gala, which meant lots of money. He didn't know a designer anything from a knockoff, but he bet that the sparkling jewels adorning women's necks were the real thing.

Moving past the registration table, his heart knocked a crooked rhythm in his chest at the thought of seeing Ripley. He knew that she would be working and wouldn't be able to get much time with him until later in the evening. Which is part of the reason for his late arrival. He also wanted to spend as little time as possible at such a formal event where he felt like an outsider. If it hadn't been Ripley asking, he would have said no to coming anywhere near something like this.

But she had outdone herself transforming a bland event

center into magic. He would give her that. Cash walked through the space, which had been draped with dark fabrics and winking lights showing through. The theme, which he read on a sign as he passed into the main ballroom, was A Galaxy Away. He knew that Ripley worked with three other people, but after seeing how she handled Emily's wedding, he could see her touch in everything. And he wasn't one to notice these kinds of details.

The main ballroom didn't have the fabric that the entry did—it was far too big—but a special lighting effect turned the ceiling of the room into a changing swirl of dark blues, purples, and a hint of iridescent pink. Tiny lights winked like stars. He felt a warm rush of pride knowing that Ripley had helped create something so magical.

But where was she?

He needed to find her. And he was also terrified to find her. Because that meant telling her everything.

Cash had already done it once, so in theory, telling Ripley about his dad and Olivia should be easier. Earlier that week, he'd finally broken down and told the guys. Who were, as he should have known, completely understanding. They listened, didn't try to give unsolicited advice, yet still somehow challenged him to work up to forgiving his father and Olivia. At the least, privately. At most, by reconciling.

"I don't think you have to do that though," Jackson had said, even as Beau looked like he wanted to protest. "I know this is a gray area for some people. But I think you can forgive someone without owing them the same relationship you had before. The boundary is yours to make. No one else can set that for you or tell you how it should be set."

It's mine to make.

Those words had given him almost as much comfort as

the ones Jackson had told him before, about how he couldn't screw things up if it was God's plan.

And while Cash had hoped that meant he could let go of the bitterness without having to talk to his father again, he knew that wouldn't be enough. The more time he spent this week working through forgiveness, praying to let go of the bitterness and anger, the more sure Cash was that he needed to reach out. He didn't know exactly what kind of relationship he would have with his father and Olivia. But he couldn't go on pretending they didn't exist.

Cash couldn't live with that. Or live with himself. As for what that meant for the future ... he would find out. After Ripley. First, he needed to mend the distance he had put between them.

At that moment, Cash caught sight of her across the room. He swallowed hard, heat moving through his chest as he watched her before she saw him. Tonight, Ripley's golden hair had been pinned up in some fancy style that Cash didn't know the name of. It lifted her hair back from her face on one side, exposing her long neck and gorgeous profile, then cascaded down on the other shoulder. He'd made the remark early on about liking her with her hair up as well as with her hair down. This showcased both perfectly.

Her gown shimmered in a color somewhere between silver and blue. Tasteful, but draped perfectly over her curves. Ripley looked great in a tacky Christmas sweater in lights. Cash actually preferred her in that level of comfort to all this formality. But the sight of her in the dress made his throat dry and his palms sweat. It transported him back to being in middle school, trying to ask Julia Riggs for the homework assignment, in a poor excuse to speak to her. He never had worked up the courage.

Tonight, he wouldn't be a coward. Tonight, he would win Ripley over, or win her back. He would put himself out there for this woman who deserved honesty and bravery—and likely, someone much better than Cash. But if she would take him, he wouldn't question whether she could do better. He would simply do his best to deserve this woman that, if he was honest, he was already falling in love with.

He began to smile as he moved across the room with singular purpose toward Ripley, realizing the full truth. He was no longer falling, present tense. He *had* fallen.

He only hoped that he hadn't already lost her.

She sensed Cash before she saw him. A prickle along her neck made Ripley turn to see him striding across the room. His eyes blazed like blue flame, scorching her with their intensity. There was a tightness to his jaw that wasn't anger but determination, she thought, as he neared her. Every cell in her body stood at attention, seemingly at his command. She couldn't even find her breath.

Guess Amber was right about the dress.

Except his eyes weren't on her dress. They were on her face, searing into her soul, and as he reached her, his presence was so large that she found herself backing into the catering person she had just been speaking to.

"Sorry," she stammered. By the gleam in her eyes, she completely understood, and disappeared through a doorway into the back with a smile.

"Can we talk?" Cash asked.

Ripley could only nod, brushing her hair behind her shoulder. As they moved out to the patio area, Amber caught her eye, giving two big thumbs up and a dimpled grin. When

Cash held the door for her, pressing his hand to the small of her back, Ripley had to resist the urge to melt into his touch. For now. Cash had things he needed to say, and she hoped that whatever they were, the end result would put her back in his arms. But just in case, she needed to guard herself. Which was hard given how amazing he looked in his tux and how good that intensity looked on him.

They made their way to a small bar-height table littered with discarded drinks and cocktail napkins. Even with the heat lamps around the patio, goose bumps popped up on Ripley's arms. Before she even realized he had taken it off, Cash draped his tux jacket over her shoulders. Her skin hummed as he lifted her hair from underneath the collar.

"Okay?" he asked.

Ripley nodded, looking away. For the past few days, she had done her best not to worry. Not to think too hard about why Cash had put up walls. She forced herself to send the occasional text, which he responded to, but barely. He didn't call. He didn't ask to see her. He had jerked the rug out from under her. She didn't want to hope for some quick fix and explanation.

Yet seeing Cash only confirmed that she had lost control of her heart days ago. Maybe it's the fact that they hit fast-forward on their relationship by having him spend so much time with her family. Maybe it was the Christmas magic in the air. But Cash held her heart in his strong hands. Ripley quaked at the thought of him letting go.

"I want to start by saying that I'm sorry I've been distant since the night at Jackson's."

Cash ran a hand through his hair, leaving it tousled in a way that made Ripley want to fix it. She balled her fists to keep from actually doing so. Maybe after this conversation. But she needed to hear him out.

"It's okay," she said.

His gaze pierced her. "Thank you, but it's really not. I needed some time to work through some things, but I could have told you that. Will you forgive me?"

"Of course."

Clearing his throat, Cash nodded. "Thank you. That night at Jackson's triggered some hard memories. There are things from my past I need to tell you. I—"

Cash paused and he pulled his cell phone from his pocket with a sigh. Ripley's stomach bottomed out. This again? She swallowed, still wanting to give him the benefit of the doubt. He set the cell phone on the table between them, and Ripley forced herself not to look at the text lighting up the screen.

Let him explain. Give him a chance.

"Two years ago, I was dating a woman named Olivia. It felt serious at the time, though now—" He shook his head. "Anyway. We'd been dating for a few months until around Christmas."

Shouts suddenly drew both of their attention to the other side of the patio. It appeared that a fight was about to break out between two men. Ripley scanned the area for security, but no one else was outside.

"I should do something about that," she said, taking a step in that direction.

"I'll handle it," Cash said. "Don't go anywhere."

He jogged over to the group, where the men's dates tried to pull them apart. Ripley felt like a mass of nerves watching Cash approach them, his hands up in a placating gesture as he stepped between the two men. Even in just his white button-down shirt and bow tie, he was an intimidating force. Still, she pulled out her cell and sent a text to Amber, asking that security be sent out to the patio. Cash seemed to be making some headway, but there was still shouting. The last thing she wanted was the event being ruined by some drunken fight, or with Cash taking a fist to the jaw because he stepped in.

When she set her phone down on the table, Cash's phone lit up. Ripley didn't mean to look. She knew that she shouldn't. But the deep-seated curiosity that comes from being human made her steal a glance. Enough to see that the text was from Olivia.

Her eyes locked on the phone. When the screen went dark, she crossed the next line of trust and picked up the phone, pressing the button to light up the screen again. It revealed the text and image that had just come through.

The picture showed a toddler, maybe a year or so younger than Tommy, as he smiled in the arms of a beautiful woman. But it wasn't the child's smile that caught her attention. It was Cash's eyes. Clearly, right there in the little boy's face. Having gone this far over the line of what was decent, she read just the excerpt showing on the still-locked screen.

Olivia: He looks so much like you and it's a reminder of all the mistakes I made. Don't make him pay for what I did. He needs you in his life. At least meet him and …

She could only read that much of the text, though it appeared there was more to read. Ripley set the phone down carefully, resisting the urge to smash the screen into the table.

Cash had a child with Olivia.

Cash was a father.

Glancing over, she could see him still dealing with the two men, who had backed down. Tension was still visible in their shoulders and jaws. Security hadn't arrived yet. Ripley didn't want to be glad, but she needed a minute. That might not be long enough.

Cash had a son. Knowing he had been that serious and that intimate with someone else made jealousy flare in her chest, an ugly emotion. It's not like she could fault him for his past. She had plenty of regrets.

None as big as deserting your own child.

To her, the idea of Cash having a child wasn't a deal-breaker. She wanted to know details and have some time to wrap her mind around this. But what kind of man had no contact with his own child? That thought had her heart curling in on itself.

Ripley struggled to control the trembling in her legs and hands. Even her lip shook, which made her realize that she was on the verge of tears. She couldn't fall apart now. She also shouldn't jump to conclusions, though the text and image seemed pretty self-explanatory.

Grasping the edge of the table, Ripley forced her shoulders back and did her best to shove the tears back. No, she would stand here and let Cash explain himself instead of running away. And if he truly was a man who would desert his own child, then she would—-

"Hey, sorry about that."

Ripley squeezed her eyes shut for a moment before looking at Cash. She couldn't meet his gaze, so settled for looking at his mouth. That was just as bad. She dropped her eyes to the ground. "You were saying?"

"Right." His fingers grazed her cheek, and she flinched. "Are you okay? You seem upset."

"I'm … I would really like for you to finish what you wanted to say." Ripley felt Cash's gaze but couldn't bring herself to look at him. It would only make it harder if she had to walk away at the end of this conversation.

"So, two years ago, I was dating Olivia. And then she told me …"

Cash broke off, the low tenor of his voice becoming more gravelly before he stopped speaking. Despite the wall she had tried to put up to guard herself, Ripley glanced up. Cash's expression haunted her. His eyes were dark, the blue almost eclipsed by his pupils, and shadowed with emotion. He ran a hand over his jaw.

Despite herself, Ripley found that she wanted to wrap her arms around him, to cup his face. Thinking about the text she read made it easier to resist.

"Go on."

He swallowed a few times, his jaw working, before he continued. "She told me that she was pregnant." His eyes flicked to Ripley, who didn't react. "You aren't surprised."

The guilt over looking at his private messages ate at her. Huffing out a breath, she said, "Fine. I looked at your phone. Olivia texted you."

Cash's brow furrowed, and he picked up his phone, typed in the passcode and read the messages. His eyes narrowed. "The phone was locked. How much of the message did you read?"

"Enough."

He shook his head and Ripley wanted to punch the hint of a smile from his face. "I'm not sure that you did. The child isn't mine, Ripley."

The words caused a cascade of emotions to ripple through her. Relief, confusion, and then a wash of empathy. "He's not?"

"No. But I'm guessing that's what you thought from seeing the text. Let me read you the rest." His eyes dropped to his phone. "'He looks so much like you and it's a reminder of all the mistakes I made. Don't make him pay for what I

169

did. He needs you in his life. At least meet him and consider having a relationship. For your brother's sake. Even if you can't forgive your father and me. I'm so sorry for how we hurt you.'"

Ripley blinked hard. "I don't understand. He's your brother?"

Cash tucked the phone back in his pocket and crossed his arms. "Olivia and my father were … together. They still are, actually. My ex is now my stepmother. That's my half brother, James."

"Oh, Cash." Ripley didn't think twice before she wrapped her arms around his waist, pressing her cheek against his warm chest. After a moment, his arms slipped underneath the tux jacket, resting on the bare skin of her back. Unsure at first, then firm. Heat from his skin passed over her in a wave. "I'm so sorry. I can't even imagine what that would be like."

"It was the worst moment of my life. I left that night and haven't seen either of them since. I've never met James. It's been eating me up inside and it's why I've been so closed off. Until you." Cash pulled back slightly so that he could see her face, his hands keeping her firmly in his grip. "I never wanted another relationship again, but something about you made me open up. Made me want more. Not just a relationship with someone but one with you, beautiful."

The tears that she'd barely held back a few minutes before slipped out. Ripley felt them, making cold tracks down her cheeks. Cash pulled his hands away from her back, brushing away her tears with his thumbs.

"That's so hard. Hard isn't even a big enough word. Are you okay?" she asked.

"I am. Well, that's not completely true. I'm on the way to okay. A work in progress. Probably a lot more work to do."

Cash wrapped his arms around her and pulled her close

again. Ripley sighed against him. "We're all just works in progress, right?"

"When Jenna made her announcement, it threw me back to Olivia telling me. I've been angry and bitter with her and my father. They did something awful, but I let it tear me apart. They've done their best to move forward from the mistakes they made. They got married. I imagine they're great parents to James. They've begged for my forgiveness. Meanwhile, I've let my anger fester. This week, that all came to a head. I've been working through it. Praying through it. I finally feel like I'm at a point where I can forgive them. Where I have forgiven them. I've let go of the bitterness. And it almost made everything okay."

"Almost?" Ripley lifted her head to look at him. Cash smiled. The first real one she'd seen on his face in almost a week. It made her stomach jump.

With one hand still on her back, the other cupped her cheek. "I met the most amazing woman. Her only flaw was that she seemed to be interested in a guy like me."

Ripley smiled, blinking back the happy tears that threatened to fall again. "Yeah? Tell me more about this flawed but amazing woman."

"Even though I was totally jaded and not interested in relationships, she got to me. Despite my rough and grumpy exterior, she liked me. I fell for her. Hard. But I couldn't keep pursuing her while holding on to all this anger. I really should have told her instead of disappearing. I guess she'll have no illusions about me being perfect."

"Not perfect. Maybe perfect for her though."

His gaze dropped to her lips. "You think so?"

"I do."

Before he could close the distance to her lips, Ripley leaned forward and fused her mouth to his. If their first kiss on Christmas Day had been a whisper, this one was a shout. Or maybe more of a chorus singing, because Ripley swore she heard music as Cash took her breath away. His hand on her back pulled her flush to him, while his other found her hair, tugging lightly in a way that lit up the nerve endings on her scalp.

Breathless, Ripley pulled back a few seconds—minutes? Hours?—later. "Wow. I think you effectively ruined me for any other kiss ever."

"I hope so. At the risk of scaring you, I'd prefer to be the last man who kisses these lips." His voice had a possessiveness to it that could have been over the top but instead filled Ripley with warmth.

"Is that a promise or a threat?"

"In your family, it seems that a pinky swear is the most binding promise."

Ripley threw her head back and laughed. It felt so good to let loose. She hadn't realized how much the waiting had weighed on her this week. "Dance with me?"

"I'm a terrible dancer. But I will for you."

"Same. Maybe we could just sway and pretend that it's a slow song, even if it's not?"

"Sounds good to me," Cash said. He pressed another quick but searing kiss to her lips, then grasped her hand firmly and led her back inside to the dance floor.

A slow song began, and Cash pulled his tux jacket from her shoulders, shrugging it back on, before his hands landed on her hips. Ripley clasped her fingers around his neck and grinned up at him. "You know, two weeks ago, I never could have imagined myself here."

"Me neither."

Her mouth kicked up in one corner. "So, you don't normally pull women over, give them a ticket, accidentally become their fake boyfriend, then ask to meet their families for real?"

"This is definitely a first." Leaning forward, his lips found her ear, his breath and his beard making shivers move down her skin. "And I really do mean it when I say I want you to be the last."

CHAPTER NINETEEN

three months later

Cash ignored the fear and nervousness rolling around in his gut. Wiping his sweaty palms on his jeans, he glanced at Ripley. Her green eyes glowed with warmth and her smile gave him the push he needed.

"Hey, buddy. Whatcha got there?" Cash knelt beside the little boy. James. *His brother*. The idea still made his head swim. Seeing him made it more than real. The pinprick of tears in his eyes evidenced just how real.

James glanced up at him, his eyes a mirror of Cash's own. They both got the blue from his dad. Their dad. This would take some getting used to. He suspected it would always be a little strange.

"Vroom." James held up a dump truck for Cash's inspection.

"That's a nice truck you've got there."

When Cash didn't take the truck, James pushed it into his hands. "You vroom."

His knees ached, so Cash sat down next to James on the rug, accepting the dump truck and diving into the imaginary world of trucks and cars. He had no idea how long they played, as he soon lost himself. When he glanced up, Ripley stood near his father and Olivia in the kitchen, watching the scene unfold.

It still stung seeing Olivia. Forgiveness or no, seeing his father and Olivia had been awkward at best. Ripley had encouraged Cash to let go of any expectations—of himself or of his father and Olivia—and let things unfold. That helped. He wasn't disappointed with how things turned out today. Maybe they would get better. Maybe not. The important thing was that Cash had come.

James, on the other hand, was easy. Cash swallowed down his regret that this was the first time he'd ever met his little brother. It made his heart ache too much to think of all the time lost. After New Year's Eve, it took Cash another few weeks to text his father back, a few more weeks after that to call, and now it was March. He had driven to Boone with Ripley beside him.

"Want to join us?" Cash held out a fire truck to Ripley. She practically ran into the room. Maybe talking to Olivia had been just as awkward for her.

"Thanks," she said softly. "I'm not jealous or anything, but it is a little weird hanging out with her."

"I know. Thank you for being here." Cash gave her a quick kiss on the cheek and watched as she entered right into James' imaginary world without any hesitations or reservations. James brightened when she suggested making a racetrack around the coffee table. When James crawled into

Cash's lap a few minutes later and fell asleep, Ripley's smile hit him solidly in the chest.

"I like this look on you," she said.

He really hoped she did. Especially considering the ring that he'd been carrying around in his pocket for the last month.

———————————

"I'd hate the winter here, but the mountains really are beautiful."

Ripley squeezed Cash's hand as they climbed the trail. She didn't want to read too much into it, but he had been quiet since they left his father's. She asked once how he thought things went, but he only said *fine*, and then stopped talking. Over the past few months, she'd learned that pushing didn't make Cash open up. Giving him space, however, did. Over time, anyway.

So, now she was doing her best to make small talk, while trying not to freak out as she waited.

"You did a really great job with James. And also with your dad and Olivia. It was awkward, but how could it not be? You were gracious and mature. I'm really proud of you."

"Thank you. I don't really want to talk about them, though. If you don't mind."

Ripley didn't mind. If she never had to have a conversation about his ex-slash-stepmother again, that would be too soon. Of course, if things stayed serious between them, that weird relationship would always be there. That's how family worked. They were who they were and you had to learn to deal with them.

If Cash was still thinking about a future with her. Normally, Ripley didn't feel the need for that kind of reassurance. But the last time she'd seen him clam up this way had been after that dinner at Jackson's where Jenna announced her pregnancy.

He's not breaking up with you, dummy. Remember how he looked at you an hour ago when you were playing with his brother.

But she couldn't help the worry from building as Cash's silence and the tension between them grew. Had something changed?

The past few months had been the best of her life. Not an exaggeration. The more Cash worked through his issues with his family, the more walls had come down. His smiles were too many to count.

"Want to stop here before we head back down?" Cash tugged her hand, moving toward a scenic overlook. An outcropping of rocks formed an edge to the trail, giving a sweeping view of the valley below.

"Are we heading back so soon?"

Cash glanced at his watch. "It's quite a drive to get back."

"Right."

Cash sat and patted the rock next to him. Ripley could practically feel the tension vibrating off him. Her own stress ratcheted up a few notches. She forced herself not to ask more questions. But she couldn't keep her mouth closed. His silent brooding drew out her awkward small talk.

"The view is really nice." Ripley would always be a beach girl over the mountains, but there was something majestic about looking down into the valley below.

"It is."

Something in Cash's voice made her turn away from the view. He smirked, his eyes fixed firmly on her face. Some of her tension evaporated as he nudged her with his shoulder. He put an arm around her, pulling her close. She would never get tired of him holding her close, or his scent that reminded her of fall days, even in the spring.

She blinked in surprise as Cash pulled away suddenly, a serious look on his face. A look that reignited her worry. Ripley crossed her arms, wishing for his warmth again as a breeze chilled her. She turned to look back over the valley, watching a slow-moving hawk circle the tree line below.

"Maybe we could go? I'm a little cold."

"I can't do this anymore," Cash said.

Ripley realized that he had gotten up and was pacing. Emotion knotted in her throat. "You can't do ... *this* anymore?"

Cash stopped, eyes wide. "Oh!" He dropped before her, grabbing one of her hands. "That came out so wrong. I'm better at handing out tickets than giving heartfelt speeches."

Before her brain could catch up to what he'd said, Ripley took in his posture. He hadn't just dropped to the ground. He was on one knee. Holding both her hands with one of his. And in the other ...

She gasped. "Is that— Are you—-?"

"Ripley Allister Johnson. Beautiful. I love you. More than I ever thought I could or would. I can't do this dating thing any longer because I want something bigger. I want every-thing with you. Though I'm sometimes still a grouch, and clearly I can't do a proposal justice, will you marry me?"

Ripley launched herself into his arms, almost taking them both down to the ground. "Yes. Yes! YES!"

His laughter rumbled against her. Cash pulled back long enough to slip the ring on her finger and kiss her into silence, his warm mouth enough to make her forget where they were.

"Oh, sorry!"

They broke apart as a voice startled them. A family with

two kids stood on the trail, staring. The mother looked like she was about to cover her daughter's eyes.

"This isn't what it looks like," Ripley started to say as Cash stood and pulled her to her feet.

"She said yes!" Cash said, lifting their joined hands to flash the ring she now wore.

The awkwardness turned into congratulations and smiles as the family wished them well before continuing on the trail.

"I feel a little like I should be carrying you down the mountain," Cash said as they started down.

Ripley giggled and leaned into his shoulder. "I think we'll be a little safer walking together. But I won't protest being carried over a threshold in a few months. Wait—how soon were you thinking we'd do this?"

Cash shot her a wide smile, the kind that still made her stomach do cartwheels. "You're the planner. If you told me tomorrow, that wouldn't be too soon. Otherwise, it's up to you. I mean, within reason. Please don't make me wait more than a year. I'll beg if I need to."

Ripley laughed, squeezing his hand as she noted the difference in weight on her ring finger. She'd hardly even glanced at the ring, only enough to know that it was a glittering, round diamond. Stunning and simple.

"A year? Nope. Too long. And there is no way I'm planning this. But I know just the right people to hire."

"Anything you want, beautiful."

"Anything? You should be careful with your promises."

"I stopped being careful when I fell in love with you. And I don't plan to start being careful now. For you, it will always be a yes."

As they made their way down the mountain trail, Ripley couldn't stop the huge smile that lit her face. Cash returned the grin, pausing at a bend in the trail to kiss her until her brain fogged.

"One," he said, when he finally pulled away.

"One?"

Cash flashed her a single finger and another brilliant smile. "One. One kiss since we've been engaged. I'm counting. Bad idea?"

Giggling, Ripley pressed a quick kiss to his lips. "Depends," she said. "How high can you count?"

THE END

That's all, folks! I hope you loved this story. If so, would you mind leaving a review? If you missed any of the other Sandover books, find them HERE.

If you loved Cash, you might really love my Not So Bad Boys series, starting with Managing the Rock Star and Forgiving the Football Player.

A NOTE FROM EMMA

I hope you loved Cash and Ripley's story! It ended up going in a different direction than I originally thought it might, as my stories sometimes do. I love Cash because I'm a sucker for the grumpy guy. And though I started dating my husband at twenty-three and married him by twenty-five, those few years between college made me understand Ripley better. It seemed like I was constantly fielding comments and expectations and set-ups from outside sources. Being single can be ROUGH! I didn't ever lie to my parents about having a boyfriend, but I don't blame Ripley. ;)

If you haven't read the others, start with Jenna and Jackson in Sandover Beach Memories, now with some BIG changes from the first edition, then Emily and Jimmy in Sandover Beach Week, and Mercer and Beau in Sandover Beach Melodies.

I'd totally move to Sandover in a heartbeat and infringe on this friend group. Wouldn't you??

Thanks so much for being a reader! If you aren't on my email list, join now for two free books (http://emmastclair.

com/freebook). In the second, you'll meet Jimmy and Emily, though it's Emily's BFF Natalie's story. You'll see the seeds of Emily and Jimmy, though, and I ended up giving them their own books because of readers telling me they needed to read their story. I also love hanging out on social media, so for a friendly reader group, come on over to my Facebook Reader group: https://www.facebook.com/groups/emmastclair/

If you haven't left a review on this book (or my others), that would mean the world to me! Thank you so much for being a reader!!

-e

Made in the USA
Columbia, SC
09 October 2020

22493811R00117